Pulp Modern

Vol. 2 No. 2 Winter 2017

Susan E. Abramski

Tom Andes

Marc E. Fitch

Matthew X. Gomez

J. Robert Kane

Preston Lang

Robert Petyo

Charles Roland

John Teel

Emile C. Tepperman

Russell Thayer

Jim Thomsen

Edited by Alec Cizak

Uncle B. Publications

Pulp Modern Vol. 2 No. 2
Published and produced by
Uncle B. Publications and Larque Press LLC

© 2017 by Alexander Cicak
Contributors retain copyright of content contributed.

Editor: Alec Cizak
Art Director: Richard Krauss
Cartoons: Bob Vojtko (p 31, 48, 100)

Printed on demand from December 2017

Printed by CreateSpace in the United States of America and other countries.

Contact information for Uncle B. Publications may be obtained through the
website: pulp-modern.blogspot.com
Contact information for Larque Press LLC may be obtained through the
website: larquepress.com

ISBN: 978-0-692-04676-0

Fiction

Classic Pulp & Editorial

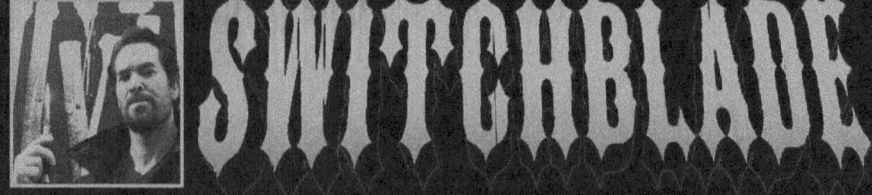

From the editor
Alec Cizak

Begin rant:

The giants rise and fall, the pillars crumble under the weight of futility, and for some reason, *Pulp Modern* marches on. The last few years have seen the loss of several crime/pulp fiction journals that had been around long before *Pulp Modern* or even *All Due Respect*, the blog I started in effort to showcase truly transgressive, politically "incorrect" fiction. Other journals have emerged, however, to fill in the gaps, though you wouldn't know it from reading recent comments on the Internet suggesting underground crime fiction is over. There's *Down & Out*, the offering from what has become the giant of independent crime fiction publishers (as far as I'm concerned), and *Switchblade*, from **Scotch Rutherford**, who wrote, in my opinion, the perfect *All Due Respect* story when ADR was still just a blog site (the story is called "Let's Make a Deal," and it's still up at the original ADR site. Go read it, I'll wait here for you).

Most recently, *Crime Factory* announced they were shutting their doors. That's a tragedy of sorts. *Crime Factory* was always an entertaining read put together by a host of talented writers. Like *Thuglit*, I considered it a bit of an institution in this "scene." I understand the 'outside' reader-base is nearly non-existent for these publications. As I often say, Oprah doesn't give a damn about us, thus, the masses don't give a damn about us. That's just the unfortunate nature of the game. As corporations have tightened their grips on all popular culture, they've brainwashed the masses into accepting whatever spineless, safe garbage they throw at them at the nearest Barnes & Noble. And B&N is participating, trust me. Any time I ask them to carry *Pulp Modern*, I'm given the same, corporate bullshit response. That response, quite simply, is code for: *You produce something we can't control. It might turn our customers into readers who can't be controlled. We can't have that. Now take your little journal-thingy and get the hell off the premises!*

My latest experience with this occurred in Missoula, where the woman in charge of determining what does and doesn't go on the shelves treated me in the same manner the principal of school 43 in Indianapolis treated me when I was in the fourth grade and tried to get my teacher fired for not following her own rules. Condescending and didactic, to be more precise. I got a taste of just how much corporate-approved writers look down on independent publishing at a reading I attended at Shakespeare and Co., an excellent independent bookstore in Missoula that's free of corporate-control and therefore stocks journals like *Pulp Modern*. So, the featured reader was a mystery writer from Whitefish. I told her about *Pulp Modern* and suggested she submit a story some time. Well, she walked right over to the shelf *Pulp Modern* sat on, picked it up, and immediately flipped to the back page. Didn't take one second to examine the writing within (was she scared?).When she saw the indication on the last page that it was a print-on-demand publication, she promptly put it back on the shelf with her nose wrinkled toward the sky in a manner suggesting she'd been asked to sniff a fresh turd. For the remainder of the evening, she ignored me, as though I had the plague and my mere presence was an offense to her lofty existence. If this is the attitude of a so-called writer, imagine how snooty the general public is when asked to give up a measly eight bucks to support the most radical writers working today.

We are at WAR. We are at war with the mundane, with the ordinary. We are at war with international corporations attempting to control the zeitgeist. I understand it's diplomatic to nod and say, "Wonderful!" every time I see the New York Times bestseller list and I see the same five names on it, over and over and over again. But I'm *not* diplomatic. I'm not "politically correct." Honesty is the precise opposite of "political correctness," and that's the venue I operate in. Corporate-controlled media is *garbage*. It's been that way since the turn of the century. This underground pulp fiction "scene" is one of the last gasps of truly independent expression. Those of you who are part of this "scene," it's time to think about new strategies to get this material to the masses. I've been told the masses will never enjoy this kind of fiction. Why? Isn't it good? Someone once said, "The crowd is a genius." Bullshit. The crowd is a moron. One, giant, collective moron. It's our job to smack the masses upside their heads and show them there are alternatives to the same, boring books being shoved down their throats at Barnes & Noble.

We can start with this issue of *Pulp Modern*, the one you hold in your hands (or are reading on your kindle device). We've got a load of crime fiction kicking things off and a nice variety of fantasy, horror, and science fiction to close it out (not getting westerns anymore at *Pulp Modern*, which is concerning). Tell your relatives, tell your lovers, tell your neighbors: New, radical, interesting fiction is alive and well, they just need to make a little effort to find it. Who knows, if we concentrate our efforts, maybe some of those pillars of the underground "scene" will make a comeback and I won't be the only one shouting my head off like a fool!

End rant.

Woe unto them who have, but do not understand, power.

Buzz Me Blues
by Russell Thayer

The girl shuddered into consciousness, unable to free her arms. The walls of a small cave or crevice held her completely. What little air she could suck at was cold, a sour stench burning her nostrils, conjuring horrors. She would die in this trap, she thought with a surge of panic, from thirst, hunger, the biting of small animals, and it wouldn't happen soon enough. Her throat cracked with dryness as she licked at the damp stone beside her head, until she realized it was the base of a toilet.

Though somewhat relieved, she still couldn't move her arms in order to extricate herself. Every portion of her body ached as she tried to twist her shoulders, pain exploding in bright light between her ears, the headache now an angry creature. She had no idea where she was or why she'd passed out in the filthy space between a wall and toilet. Dawn had not come quite yet, but enough urban radiance came through the window that she could make out the small hexagonal tiles in front of her face. It wasn't her own bathroom, that much she knew. With a probing effort, her bare feet found and gripped the cold iron base of a radiator, and with harsh grunting she gradually pulled her thin torso from the cramping space. Sitting up finally, her back against the wall, she wanted very much to go home.

Her brain throbbed less as the blood drained out of it, and she began to collect information. Her new cotton blouse was completely unbuttoned. She felt inside. Whoever had done that had stopped at her brassiere, not enough meat behind the plain cotton cups to interest most men. Her best skirt was bunched around her waist, the chill of tile against her bottom telling her she'd been separated from her underpants. She leaned to look into the toilet, fought the urge to gag, then pulled the handle, making a clunk and a rush of noise. A drink of water would

be very nice, she thought, not sure if she could ever get to her feet again. A sink hung from the wall only a few feet away. She would work out a plan about how to get over there.

Where was she? What had she done? What had been done to her? Lifting the skirt over her waist, the girl felt between her legs. She could guess at least one man had been there, but she didn't feel she'd been used as a playground. There was no pain, no blood. She was not a maiden at twenty, nor much of a complex moralist. *People should get what they deserve*, she often preached, but that didn't mean she thought she deserved to have a baby at this point in her life. She wasn't stupid. Not usually, anyway.

Then she remembered the party. The agent's party. This was his apartment, and she'd been very stupid. She closed her eyes, recalling the close press of men in silk shirts, dancing, the turntable spinning at full volume, the drinking of strong cocktails much too quickly. It seemed so long ago, the night before, hours before, when her skin twitched with nervous excitement after climbing four floors to the address written on the back of a coaster in her pocket, following the laughter and music, confronted by the reeling man, a talented clarinetist she recognized, who rushed out the door at her, touching her red hair, suggesting she should run for her life if she knew what was good for her. Why was she still here?

This whole mess had started the weekend before, at the Town Club, during one of its celebrated Sunday jam sessions. Vincent, a drummer she'd let kiss her once for ten minutes in Mrs. Bragana's apartment before the woman came home and threw him out on his ear, had dragged her down to the joint, confronting the owner, demanding she be allowed to sit in at the piano for one set. The musicians all complained, eyes rolling, but gave in after Vince paid for a tray of beers. In time they waved her up, a harmless novelty, a young white woman on stage at one of San Francisco's top jazz venues, where nine tenths of the men drinking in the shadows had skin as black as burnt wood. It hadn't taken long for her to become over-animated at the attention she received, full of sparkling beer herself, sometimes standing at the piano as she sailed through her solos, comping for the others when they took off, often receiving a wink or a grin after some sweet voicings. They never cared to ask her real name, which was Maggie, but she glowed with affection at the pet names they did try out: *Miss Firecracker, Little Red Rocket,* finally settling on *Sparky.* When she tripped back to her booth for a breather, the agent was there, giving her a silent handclap as she wiggled onto the bench, more than a little drunk, her brain alive with the heady sensation of fitting in, watching the older men play, knowing she could run with them.

"Miss Bates," he'd said, his hand on her knee, "you make my head spin."

And then the real intoxication began, the 90-proof stuff, the heaping praise she'd been craving. She was ready for it, and the agent dribbled it over her with a spoon, thick as honey, and she lapped it up like a child with a sweet tooth, smiling back at him, her eyes encouraging the agent to find her a job doing the one thing she loved.

Well, this wasn't going to be her job, Maggie thought as she turned her tired body onto her knees, pulling herself to her feet using a well-anchored towel bar. If she'd led the agent on, it wasn't as though she expected this very thing to happen. She filled her cupped fingers with cool water, wiping a wet hand across her taut forehead. She tried to avoid the insipid face in mirror, but her eyes couldn't avoid themselves, and she noted the weariness, the cheeks with their childish freckles, the disheveled red madness she flattened with wet hands and tucked behind the delicate ears she thought her best feature.

"Miss Bates," she told the girl in front of her, "I don't like you very much."

Opening the door to the medicine cabinet, her disagreeable features evaporating, she fumbled among the razor blades and hair tonic, looking for aspirin, Benzedrine, anything to make her head loosen its tight cords. After she closed the door, that girl was there again, staring back at her.

"Where are your socks and shoes?" she asked.

The bathroom door stood closed, and she dreaded the scene on the other side of it. With a deep breath she slowly turned the knob.

Dim light faded to her end of the hallway. She crept along the wall toward the living room, where one lamp burned, lying on its side. The room had exploded, the dense crowd of people blown completely away. She had a garbled memory of sitting on the couch, giggling between two Negroes as they put a needle into her arm.

"What if the police come?" she remembered asking. The party was loud enough. One of the men, a thin mustache, told her to relax.

"Ain't nobody gonna' call the po-leece," he assured her as he loosened the rubber tube high on her arm, making her whimper as she sank into the deep cushions without a thought in her head, the wash of feeling more intense than when she pleased herself, just so, with her own strong fingers. Those cushions had now been thrown in all directions, every lamp knocked over, their shades removed and flattened.

The bedroom door stood open. Maggie could only imagine

passing through it as she stumbled to the bathroom at some point during the night, remembering nothing after the jolt of dope. The agent lay on his bed, satisfied, filled to bursting with her, stinking of sweat. He was older than she remembered, the thick hair on his chest mostly gray against the pink sheets. A pillow slumped against the wall. One of her saddle-shoes had crept with shame under a wooden chair. The agent's snoring made her think of a Sherman tank crawling on concrete, and she remembered the prison camp again, and the day of her liberation, the Jap guards beaten to death by men and women she thought she'd known, and how promising the future seemed once she was free. She looked at the pillow on the floor and wondered if she'd be able to hold it over the agent's face until the snoring stopped. Would he ever try to find her a gig now that he'd gotten what he wanted? Not unless she went with him again, her eyes open this time, telling him how much she liked it.

The small kitchen was devoid of anything domestic, just empty beer bottles. There were no cooking utensils, no pans, lids, not even a box of crackers. It was a cheap apartment rented solely for the debasement of eager young women, and she hated it for that, for what it had seen, and might yet see again.

Remembering a story once told to her by a very questionable character, Maggie went to the stove and blew out the pilot lights at each burner. She turned the control knobs until gas hissed out.

After propping open the swinging kitchen door with a chair, she returned to the bedroom. The hacking snore continued, comically, and she was suddenly no longer afraid of or in awe of his power. He was just a man. After pulling the sheet away from his waist, she stared down at the heavy gut and wilted penis. He stank of sweat, and there was much too much hair everywhere. She nodded. He'd had her, and that was something she could never undo. Her underpants were visible under his calf. She tugged the plain white pants away, shoving the wadded clump into the pocket of her skirt, sorry he wouldn't remember his beloved *Sparky*. After collecting her shoes and socks, she sat in the hard chair to slip them on, no longer looking at the man in the bed.

In the living room, the girl found her leather flight jacket by the side of the couch. She was happy to wriggle into the familiar skin. The room wore a chill now, its two large windows wide open, gulping fresh air. After one last tour of the apartment, closing all the windows, setting the overturned telephone back on its table, making sure the line was in service, she let herself out, the mounting odor of gas now beginning to make her queasy.

At an Italian coffee shop across the street, the girl ordered espresso from her seat at the counter. A clock told her it was almost six-thirty. There were no other customers. The owner set a tiny cup in front of her, asking if she was all right, if she wanted a pastry on the house, but she ignored him, poking in the zippered interior pocket of her jacket for coins, laying a quarter on the counter. The man set a plate with a warm buttered roll on the counter in front of her, telling her to eat. After making a face, she took a bite, noticing a phone booth at the rear of the cafe. She looked at the clock again, feeling in her side pocket for a smoke. After swallowing the espresso, her head just beginning to feel better, the girl lit her first cigarette of the day. She would sit there for a half hour, thinking a lot, working out how she'd never let a night like this happen again. She knew she could play the piano well enough to make money at it. Anywhere, at any time. Since the age of nine, with her father's encouragement, she'd been neglecting her classical studies in order to play the various shades of blue he loved. She could knock out a Chopin piece from memory if required to, but the innovative sounds of 1948 gave her an even bigger thrill. It had been her father's dream for his little girl to lead her own band one day, like Lillian Armstrong. The girl wasn't against the idea.

Her day would come, but it wouldn't come the way the hungry agents thought it should. She'd continue to steal every new jazz recording she could lay her hands on. She'd continue to jam at the clubs, gaining experience, letting them see what a girl could do when she got the chance. Something would happen. She'd have to keep waitressing for now, maybe find a young student or two for Saturday afternoons. She'd have to earn her own money if the agents wouldn't help her, and she'd have to

stay away from men and beer, and never put that stuff in her arm again, no matter how thoroughly it blotted out the things she'd seen. After she made a success of herself, when people paid money to hear her play, then she might let the right man fall in love with her. Or she might rather grow old alone, in a lovely apartment full of fine books and records, with a good piano at the ready, billowing curtains, and a view of the bay in sunshine. She hoped she wasn't pregnant.

Thinking was hard work, and the girl asked for another espresso. Time passed with more cigarettes. She glanced at the clock. That ought to do it.

After closing the door of the phone booth, the cafe owner watching her with concern, the girl pulled the coaster from her pocket. The agent's telephone number had been scribbled on the back in pencil, just under the bar's address. She dialed the number, waiting, imagining the ball of electricity shooting down the line to spark at the other end. It was a good trick, she thought, smiling as she leaned against the polished wooden wall.

After a few seconds, the pane of glass rattled weakly in the phone booth door. The owner ducked silently, his head turning with alarm to stare in shock out the window at something calamitous across the street. A woman rushed into the coffee shop, her face white with fear. It all played out like a silent movie.

After placing the handset back in the cradle, the girl stepped out of the phone booth.

As she walked toward the door, the owner raised his hand, advising her to stay off the street, that there was a fire in a nearby building.

"I'll be OK," she said, flipping him a dime. "That's for the bread roll."

Russell Thayer holds a BA in English from the University of Washington. He is a retired printer and lives in Montana with his wife and dog.

Only the patient succeed at a trade as particular as crime.

Black Lab
by Jim Thomsen

The three men had just taped the last plastic sheet to the last window in the house when Hartsock felt his phone vibrate through the pocket of his hazmat suit. The blood in his face seemed to drop twenty degrees as he read the text message.

"Oh, no," he breathed. "They're coming back."

"What?" Coop said as he struggled into his own suit and shot a look at Rhatigan, who fixed Hartsock with feral red eyes up as he wheeled in the barrel of anhydrous ammonia. A box of Erlenmeyer flasks wobbled atop it.

"The Kostoffs. The homeowners?" Hartsock said. "You're not going to believe this. They forgot the baby's diaper-rash lotion."

"Are you fucking kidding me?" Rhat said. "They can't just stop at the fucking Rite Aid?"

"Tear down while you talk." Hartsock was already ripping at the translucent plastic. "It's prescription stuff, I guess. I don't know. All I know is that we've got maybe ten minutes."

"There's just no way." Rhat pulled a handgun from the back of his pants. "There's not enough time."

"Put that away," Hartsock said as he balled up a medicine-ball-sized wad of plastic. He kept his voice even, but he had a shit-his-pants-in-the-next-six-seconds feeling. Rhat not only wanted to be a badass, he wanted to be in charge. He was neither. He had the criminal resumé and the connections, but Hartsock had the housesitting cover and the chemical know-how, and ultimately his proposal was the one backed by the guys from Sinaloa, who were eager to expand into new territory and were smart enough to appreciate that with fewer Mexican faces in this suburban town, fewer questions were likely to be asked.

That limited the supply of local talent, however, and that raised the ambition of the talent Hartsock could scratch up through the few connections he made during the one stretch in the county jail that quietly killed his corporate chemical-engineer career. That ambition made Rhat dangerous, and Hartsock wondered if it came from being a guy who looked like he fit his name, like a cross between Steve Buscemi and a California raisin. Or being a penis-sized guy who spent two-plus years in Pelican Bay for possession with intent and probably got passed around like a pucker-holed piñata from one Aryan Nation potentate to the next.

Either way, Rhat had too much to prove, and if bullets went flying at some point, Hartsock had little doubt that one of them would have his name on it.

"Stuff the plastic in the pantry," Hartsock said, nodding toward the stairs. "They won't go in there."

"Sho nuff, Boss Man." Rhat said in a Stepin Fetchit voice. He snapped off a mock salute with the barrel of his gun. "But if this goes south, whatever I gotta' do is on you." He gave Hartsock his best fuck-your-mother stare, which actually wasn't half-bad as fucked mothers go. But Hartsock managed to keep his eyes steady, and after several seconds Rhat tucked the gun back in his belt and stepped to the wall. Coop three-pointed the hand truck and headed back to the garage.

Hartsock breathed a little easier as his bowels backed down to DEFCON 2.

Ten minutes later, Hartsock watched from the living-room window as Coop backed out of the driveway in the panel van with the housepainter logo on the sides. Rhat, muttering black murder every step of the way, had just shut himself inside the pantry with the plastic.

Seconds later, a maroon minivan turned onto Pine Butte Crest.

Hartsock had just peeled off the last of the painter's tape—or so he hoped—when the keys rattled at the front door and Linda Kostoff stepped in. "I'm so sorry, John. We seem to have our heads up our . . . bottoms, this morning." She gave out a breathy little laugh. "I'd have just run to Rite Aid, but nothing seems to work on Tucker as well as the sixty-dollars-a-tube stuff."

"No problem at all," Hartsock said, and worked up a stretch of his lips that he hoped passed for a smile. "Just thinking of cooking up a little something."

"Oh, well, you're welcome to the last of the spinach-lentil soup in the fridge," Linda said as she headed toward the baby's room. "We made way too much of it the other night. I keep forgetting how finicky Trent Junior is. He just wants corn dogs for breakfast, lunch and dinner."

"I'm on his side," said Hartsock, who loved corn dogs, and

was lucky enough to have the high-octane metabolism to ride them out.

"Great. You're fired," said Linda as she scurried back into the living room. "Seriously, you're our favorite housesitter. I'm so glad your mom suggested you, and so glad you're always available on short notice. Thanks so much for taking care of our . . ." She stopped. "Where's Doolittle?"

Hartsock's insides turned to liquefied corn dogs. He'd forgotten about the dog. He'd had Coop stash the Kostoff's black Labrador in the back of the van because the dog wouldn't stop barking at Rhat, and Rhat wouldn't stop threatening to shoot the dog in the face. Hartsock's widowed mother had a big backyard and had agreed to look after Doolittle for the long weekend, no questions asked. Well, not exactly no questions asked — a lot of questions asked, actually — but a hundred bucks and a bottle of Bombay Sapphire bought her grudging silence.

"Uhhhh. She's in the backyard. Saw a squirrel run up a tree a few minutes ago, I think."

Linda gave Hartsock a long look. "I don't hear her barking."

"I, uh. I can go check," Hartsock said, and made for the back door.

"Usually she barks up a storm when she hears the minivan coming," Linda said.

"I'll go see what's up," Hartsock said, sliding open the door, not knowing what he was doing beyond hoping that Rhat wasn't racking the slide on his gun.

Linda studied Hartsock's face for another long few seconds. Then waved her hand and headed for the front door. "It's OK. I trust you. I don't want to keep Trent and the kids waiting. Just don't let her go on barking and bother the neighbors, OK?"

"Sure thing," Hartsock said. "I never want to attract the notice of the neighbors."

Linda gave him a tight, distracted smile and promised not to bother him again. A minute later Hartsock waved to the Kostoffs from the doorway as the minivan backed again onto Pine Butte Crest.

"Is that mouthy bitch gone yet?" Rhat said, poking his head out from the pantry door.

"Shut up. She's nice. I like her."

"Why? You want to fuck her?" Rhat stepped out, gun in hand. He held it high and pumped his hips. "Oh, Hartie Boy, rip off my mom jeans! Pour oaky chardonnay all over my ass and lick it off! Hurry, before I have to meet the girls for book club!"

Hartsock gave him his best I'm-not-gonna-dignify-that-comment look. "Put that gun away. And call Coop and tell him to turn around right now. He can take the dog to my mom's later. We're already behind."

"You call him, Boss Man. I'm going to take a shit." Rhat strode down the hall before Hartsock could respond.

Twenty minutes later, Hartsock, Rhat and Coop were setting up the last of the folding tables when Hartsock's phone buzzed again. He reached into his pocket as Rhat gave him an apocalyptic eye roll.

The text read: *Sorry again! We forgot Trent Jrs game iPad and he's pitching a fit! Back in 15!*

Hartsock didn't read the text aloud, but he didn't have to. Rhat read his face.

"You. Have. Got. To Be. Fucking. Kidding Me." Again, Rhat pulled the handgun from the back of his pants. "I am not tearing this shit down again. We're ready to rock this cook." Behind him, Coop, who was threading copper tubing onto the condensation flasks, looked from Rhat to Hartsock and nodded. He always looked to Rhat first, Hartsock was noticing, as if Rhat were the one calling the shots.

"If they come through this door, I'm going to do what I have to do," Rhat continued. "A choice between them or us is no choice at all."

"Quit being such a tough guy," Hartsock said, massaging the mounting headache spreading from his sinuses. "You are not killing a family of four. You're not killing anyone."

"At least I'm willing to. Are you?" Rhat made a show of popping the magazine, studying it, and popping it in again. Hartsock guessed that Rhat had seen the move in a Nicolas Cage movie. Probably the same one from which he got ninety percent of what came out of his ratlike mouth.

"Look, just relax," Hartsock said. "I'll find out where it is, and meet them in the driveway. Just pull the sheeting off the front windows."

"Pull it down yourself, asshole."

"Jesus, just do it, all right?" Hartsock stepped into the hall and sent the text. He waited an agonizing few minutes until the reply came: *THX! He says he left it on the desk in his rm. Mybe the bkshelf?*

It took five frenetic minutes, but he found the device under Junior's bed, next to a small riot of crusted Go-Gurt containers. When he returned to the living room, the sheeting was still up over the windows. He started to tell Rhat again to take it down, but the other man gave him a strange, milky gaze and looked away. Hartsock tugged at the tape in one corner and flinched a little as Rhat's shrill chuckle sounded behind him.

Five minutes later, Hartsock stepped into the drive as the Kostoff's van pulled up once more. He arranged the lines of his sweat-sheeted face into his best facsimile of a smile.

"What do you say to the nice housesitter, Trent?" Linda said as she handed back the tablet that Hartsock passed through the window. The boy, six or seven at most, mumbled something and his dad offered an embarrassed grin. "Well, I for one thank you," Trent Sr. said. "I'd rather listen to country music than to Trent without his favorite game, and I'd rather shoot myself in the face than listen to country music."

"I'm here to help," Hartsock said.

Trent Sr. flashed Hartsock a harried Philip Seymour Hoffman grin. "OK, we'd better go before they give away our campsite." He dropped the minivan into reverse and looked dramatically at the car roof. "I promise, this is it. Please, dear God, let this be it."

Hartsock silently seconded that emotion.

Ten minutes later the three men were fully zipped into their suits and helmets and ready, in Rhat's words, to make rocks and roll.

Hartsock's phone buzzed once more.

This time he didn't stop what he was doing or look at Rhat. Rhat had already broken a beaker and was bitching about how hard it was to hook up the coils through his gloved fingers. Any further setbacks would shove him over the edge. Or give him the pretext he thought he needed to take over. Probably in a way Hartsock would never see coming.

It was seven or eight minutes later, when the first batch was underway, that Hartsock finally stepped back and took off his hood long enough to announce that he needed to take a leak. Coop didn't look up. Rhat gave a dismissive flip of his hand.

Hartsock walked past the fireplace mantel on which Rhat had set his handgun. In the bathroom, he pulled off his gloves and pulled out his phone with a cold, damp hand.

You're gonna hate us! But Trent thinks he forgot his gun. He's worried about mtn lions! Can you believe??? 10 mins max!

His fingers shook as he tapped out his reply: *Can I grab it for you?*

The reply quickly came: *Locked in a gun safe in the bedrm. Only T knows combo.*

Hartsock closed the phone and caught a glimpse of his gray, papery face in the medicine-cabinet mirror.

He didn't want to admit it. But Rhat was right.

A choice between them or us was no choice at all.

He mopped his face, eyes lost and afloat in their sockets like . . . well, the eyes of a meth-head. He didn't touch the stuff himself, though he didn't deny being tempted. But he suspected that Rhat did. You didn't get teeth, or a temperament, like Rhat's from drinking too much coffee or smoking too many Camels.

He returned to the living room. Rhat gave him the briefest of glances. The instant Rhat turned back to the cook, Hartsock swept his hand behind him and picked up Rhat's weapon. He'd never fired a weapon before, but some reptilian part of his brain told him that Rhat wasn't the kind of guy who bothered to put the safety on.

He was right.

Rhat never saw the shot coming.

Rhat dropped, just like that, magenta mind mist splattering all over the sheeting like a highly pixelated piece of modern art. Hartsock's breath hitched, for just a second, and then he felt rather than saw Coop's eyes jerk up from the evaporator he had been diligently monitoring. He turned.

"Jesus" was all Coop managed to huff through the hood before Hartsock put a bullet right in the middle of it.

Hartsock stared at both bodies for a few hot buzzing seconds before taking the deepest breath of his life and putting the gun against his own head.

Then the phone in his pocket vibrated once more. He ignored it as he stared through the sheeting over the living-room window, waiting for the impressionistic maroon blur of the Kostoff's minivan to darken the driveway once more. It kept not happening, and Hartsock kept not shooting himself in the head. So he figured he might as well read the message before pulling his plug.

Never mind! Trent forgot that he packed the gun in his backpack last nite! Sorry! You're so awesome to put up with us. We're such a bunch of goofy scatterbrains! Bye!

Hartsock looked at the scattered brains of his two colleagues. Then, as the sirens in his ears finally began to silence, he heard the shrill barking of a dog pinballing off the walls. Doolittle. In the garage. In the van. He headed toward the basement stairs, thinking of the dog. And the chainsaw hanging on the wall of the garage. And how a little barking in the backyard might provide the cover he needed to cut up the bodies of his colleagues. If he made it quick.

For that, he'd need the help of coffee and corn dogs. And whatever crank he could find in Rhat's coat pockets. Then he'd carry on with the cook. "The Sinaloa show must go on," he said with a shaky, splintery laugh, as he descended.

Jim Thomsen is a manuscript editor, bookseller, copywriter and house-sitter based in his hometown of Bainbridge Island, Washington. He spent nearly 25 years as a newspaper reporter and editor. His short fiction has been accepted for publication in *West Coast Crime Wave*, *Shotgun Honey* and *Switchblade*, but his biggest claim to published fame might be turning up as a character in the C.J. Box thriller *Pardise Valley*. For more about Jim, check out jimthomsencreative.com and follow his noir photography on Instagram.

Sometimes, following your dreams means stepping over a dead body or two.

After Midnight at the C'est La Vie Lounge

by Tom Andes

After three days holed up in his room at the Deauville, watching basic cable and eating delivery from Happy Garden, Gardner couldn't take it anymore. Tuesday, he walked next door to the C'est La Vie Lounge and ordered a shot of Jack, Budweiser back. Touching the bottle to his brow, he closed his eyes and saw the face of the pimp he killed in New Orleans, the flare of the muzzle illuminating the guy's molars through his cheeks. How long before the mobster named Leon Hayes or the cops came for Gardner?

Later, he couldn't say which one of them initiated the conversation. Last thing he remembered was leaving the place, and he woke here: yellow sheets on a full-sized mattress with thin pillows and no headboard, in a cluttered bedroom with a mahogany dresser, somewhere (he guessed) outside Thibodaux.

Gardner sat up, head pounding. He felt like prey—abject, desperate, and hunted. Nearby, in another house, a radio played the new Lauryn Hill, "Doo Wop (That Thing)," which the girl in New Orleans liked. A gold crucifix hung by the door. He rubbed his face, closed his eyes, and saw the dead man, his brains spilling out the top of his head where he lay on the Mississippi River levee. *What hope do I have of redemption?*

He found his clothes on the floor.

He wasn't aware of hearing the shower until it stopped. His skin slick with sweat, he climbed out of bed.

When the woman came in the room, wrapped in a towel, he shoved her up against the wall.

"What do you want from me?"

He couldn't remember her name. But Hayes was connected to the State Line Mob and the Dixie Mafia, and he could reach you anywhere. Why not through her, here?

She had blond highlights. She clawed his arm, her brown eyes wide, frantic. He relaxed his grip. *What am I doing?* Breath rattled her windpipe. He repeated the question, and she shook her head, her long neck straining.

"Do you know someone named Leon Hayes?" Gardner watched her eyes, but he didn't think he'd be able to tell if she were lying. Could never tell with a woman. The guy he killed worked for Hayes, who Gardner glimpsed once from a distance. "He's a big guy with a handlebar mustache, a gangster from the Irish Channel. He's killed dozens of people—maybe hundreds."

Turned just in time to avoid the knee she aimed at his crotch. Her heel caught his shin, fingernails swiping his cheek. He swore, surprised by her strength.

When he released her, she fell to the floor. On hands and knees, still wrapped in her towel, she retched. Gardner sat on the bed. His cheek stung, but when he touched it, wasn't any blood. On the opposite side of the room, a boot—too large to be hers—lay on its side.

"You're married." That came back to him. She started crying. "What's the matter with you?" She rubbed her collarbone. "I was going to make you breakfast."

"Where's your husband?"

Like he needed any more enemies. The night he left New Orleans, a pasty-faced Irishman came for him, and Gardner went out the window of his rented room, catching a glimpse of a second man, who he could only assume was Hayes, through a chain link fence before fleeing across an abandoned lot. Silhouetted by streetlights, Hayes stood in the exhaust of a Trans Am, mutton chop sideburns hanging from his jowls.

"He works offshore," she said. "I told you last night."

"What do you want from me?" He was beginning to think she didn't know Hayes at all.

"What did you think I wanted last night?"

Gardner rubbed his eyes. "What's your name?"

Her chin lifted. "It's Krystal. I told you that, too."

Gardner fastened his belt. The radio had stopped. "I have to go."

At the foot of the driveway, cars hurtled past on a two-lane state highway. Gardner stood by the road, jingling the coins in his pockets, wondering how he looked to passing drivers, those suckers going to work on a Wednesday morning, straight johns in a world he'd given up belonging to. He was a killer: ruthless, coldblooded, and without conscience. He felt queasy—and the heat didn't help.

"Where the hell am I?" he said aloud. He didn't know the way back to Thibodaux. He pulled a dime from his pocket and flipped it, the silver winking in the sunlight. Heads. He started up the road in the direction of a railroad trestle.

Must've rained during the night. Alongside the highway, gnats swarmed over drainage channels, and runoff pooled on the lawns.

A horn sounded. A beige Buick pulled up. Krystal leaned across the front seat and lowered the passenger's window. "I'd be happy to give you a lift."

Air conditioning leaked from the car—a relief. He rested his hands on his knees, stooping to peer in the window. "You don't have any idea who I am."

"I didn't know who you were last night, either." A strand of blond hair stuck to her cheek. "You didn't have any call to go storming out of my house."

Christ, he didn't envy the woman's husband.

"I didn't storm. I left."

"You should know if you're trying to go back to the motel, it's that way." She pointed over her shoulder with her thumb.

"Sure you don't work for Hayes?"

He knew better. But he didn't want to owe anybody.

"Honey, I don't know the first thing about Hayes. And really, if I meant you any harm, I could have done whatever I wanted to do to you last night. You're a pretty sound sleeper, least when you're drunk."

Gardner grunted.

"Come on." Krystal slapped the passenger seat. She reached up and tugged on the handle of the door, which fell open, bumping his knees. "I won't bite, not unless you ask."

His shoulders slumped in defeat. There seemed no escaping the woman. Gardner climbed in the car. In the next driveway, Krystal turned around, piloting the Buick back the way they came.

Gardner adjusted the vents so the air conditioning was blowing on his face. Krystal slouched, craning her neck to see over the wheel. Outside town, they passed a used car lot.

When they pulled up in front of the Deauville, the parking lot was empty. Sunlight blanched the gravel. Behind a fence, fake palms cast stingy shadows over the pool.

"I going to see you again?" Krystal sat with her hands on her thighs.

"What about your husband?"

She was wearing a peach-colored skirt and a sheer white top. Her cheeks had gone red in the heat. She was his age, 24—too young to be tied down to a guy she didn't even like. "Things aren't going well with my husband."

"I don't want to get in the middle of that." Made that mistake in New Orleans, getting between a girl and the guy who was pimping her, only to discover the girl didn't want to be protected, so Gardner ended up here, on the run, broke. The girl claimed to be Hayes' niece, which meant Hayes should have been grateful to Gardner, instead of wanting him dead. Showed you what came of helping people.

"Billy comes back in two weeks. If you need to disappear when he does, I'll understand."

"That your husband's name?"

She licked sweat from her lip. "If that's the only thing about him you ever know, that would be fine with me."

Gardner already knew too much. He opened the door, one foot on the gravel, and the other still in the Buick.

"This was my granddaddy's car." She gave a helpless laugh. "The seat's busted. I'm five eight, and I can barely see to drive."

She sounded like a kid, which made him feel sorry for her. Leaning back in the car, Gardner fished a ballpoint from the coffee cup in the console. "Write your number on something."

Krystal scrawled the digits across his palm. "You weren't planning on sticking around much longer, anyway, were you?"

"I guess not."

"Might as well have some fun while you're here."

No intention of seeing her again, but Gardner told her his room number and closed the door. She pulled out of the lot, the Buick's tires kicking up dust.

In his room, he splashed cold water on his face and dried with a towel. From the suitcase in the corner, he took a clean undershirt. He hung the shirt he was wearing over the back of the chair to dry.

Unzipping the lining of the suitcase, he extracted a pile of bills and counted them into stacks on the bed: 400 bucks, which was all the cash he brought with him when he left New Orleans, less the money he spent on this room, on Chinese delivery, and last night at the bar. He folded 300 bucks into his trousers and zipped the remaining hundred back into the suitcase. If he could get to Houston, Hayes couldn't touch him.

From the desk drawer, he took the Beretta and sniffed the barrel, but he detected no trace of cordite, nothing to reveal the weapon had been fired four days ago. He popped the clip, which was missing one round, and reinserted it. His hands steady, he sighted down the barrel at the mirror on the other side of the room.

"I'm a killer." He repeated the sentence. He felt sick. On the muzzle of the gun, the man he murdered left two silver nicks barely visible in the bluish sheen when he clamped down with his teeth. Just before Gardner pulled the trigger, the man begged for his life, saliva bubbling around the barrel of the gun.

Before he shot the pimp, Gardner had never killed anybody. Up to that point, he was strictly low-level; an errand boy, running numbers. Well, he'd graduated.

He flicked the safety off and on. With the weapon in the back of his trousers and the small of his back slick with sweat, he put his shirt on, letting the tails dangle over the butt of the gun. He walked across the room, inspecting himself in the mirror. A telltale bulge remained.

"Shit." His jacket was draped over the armchair next to the window. "I'm not wearing a jacket in this heat," he said.

Gardner pulled the gun and dropped it back in the desk drawer. Standing in front of the window unit, he let the air conditioning cool his armpits. He peered around the edge of the blind, but the lot was empty.

He had two books: *The Notorious Jumping Frog of Calaveras County and Other Stories* and *The Fire Next Time*, both of which he'd stolen, picking them at random from a bookshop on Magazine before he fled New Orleans. He tried reading them, but after 20 pages of each, couldn't remember a word.

He left the gun in the drawer, the books on the table next to the bed.

A mile and a half up the road, a knoll rose from the swampland. On it perched the town of Thibodaux, a cluster of brick buildings around a courthouse and a small grid of shaded residential streets with names familiar to Gardner from his time in New Orleans: St. Charles, General Nicholls. Half a mile beyond that, Gardner found the used car lot he passed with Krystal that morning. He probably could have stayed here, at least for a day or two, but he wanted to get moving before the people who were after him caught up to him.

By the time Gardner pulled up in front of the Deauville in a gray '78 Chevy van he bought for three hundred, cash, it was a quarter of six. A muted orange skyline the color of a melted creamsicle silhouetted the trees. The engine rattled to a stop.

Gardner climbed out of the van. The Buick was parked in front of the C'est La Vie.

"Shit." He planned on leaving town that evening. If she saw the van, he would have to explain himself. He wasn't any good at talking to a woman, especially not when he had to tell her something she didn't want to hear. Far easier when you were saving them or screwing them.

He crossed the lot and put his key in the lock on his motel door.

Before he could turn the knob, the door fell away from him, swinging open onto blackness.

Half blind from the sunlight, Gardner blinked and waited for his eyes to adjust. His suitcase had been emptied on the bed, the desk drawer opened, his books tossed across the floor. He never should have told her his room number—but how did she get in his door?

He lunged inside. He glanced in the bathroom, looking for Krystal. He picked up his jacket.

"Stop right there," a man's voice said.

A guy appeared behind the door. He wore a gray Motörhead tee shirt with holes in the armpits, and he pointed a pistol at Gardner's face. Graying mutton chop sideburns hung from the man's jowls—the same guy who was standing behind the Trans Am a few nights ago. He had a handlebar mustache. A white dude, but when he grinned, his gold teeth shone.

"The hell are you doing here?" Gardner backed toward the door, though he knew who the guy was, and what he was doing there, too. He came to kill Gardner.

Another man appeared behind the bathroom door.

"Hey," he said.

The same guy came to Gardner's room the other night.

Gardner backed out of the room. In the first man's hand, next to Gardner's ear, the pistol cracked. Behind Gardner, the windshield of the van exploded. Deafened, Gardner dropped his room key, covering his ear, and fell to his knees. The man was laughing.

"Not so fast," he said.

A second shot flattened the right rear tire of the van.

Stumbling to his feet, Gardner braced himself against the doorframe. Pushing off against the wood, he ran.

"He missed." Gardner flailed his arms as he fled across the parking lot in the waning heat, though even as he said it, he knew the man wasn't aiming for him. Why not? "Missed," Gardner repeated, not daring to look over his shoulder as he ran in the direction of the swamp, and the new subdivisions behind the motel.

Gardner reached a drainage canal at the edge of a sugarcane field when he heard a car engine. As he emerged from between the stalks, the sharp edge of a leaf caught him across the face, slicing his cheek. Ten yards ahead, the rutted gravel road ended, tumbling down an incline and into a black trench of water. When he touched his cheek, blood stained the heel of his hand.

"Son of a bitch."

He crawled toward the canal. One man crashed through the sugarcane, the other one coming down the road, waving a pistol out the window of that red Trans Am. Dust billowed from under the tires.

"He's up here," one shouted.

"Got him," came the response.

One whooped.

Gardner couldn't have said what stopped him from jumping in. Kneeling at the edge of the canal, he only knew that whatever drove him from New Orleans to Thibodaux, Louisiana, had run its course. He didn't like the water. Like a woman—like Krystal, like the girl he was stupid enough to try to protect in New Orleans—its surface seemed to mask hidden depths. Falling though the trees, the evening sunlight set fire to the canal.

"No you don't, buddy," a voice said behind him in a brogue.

But Gardner wasn't going anywhere. Standing on his knees, he clasped his hands behind his head. After they shot him, they would kick his body into the canal, and so much the better. He felt warmth on his leg, something trickling across the gravel by his knee.

"Oh God," he said.

He wet himself.

I guess I'm a coward, after all. Fine. He relaxed his bladder, letting piss wash down his thighs, waiting for the absolution death might bring.

"Just get it over with," he said.

Something hit him between the shoulder blades, and he pitched forward, brambles scratching his cheeks, face-first onto the embankment over the water. *Here it comes,* he thought, and a pair of hands rolled him onto his back to look at the sky one last time, at the jet trails seeming to make a perfect letter X across the blue. A pale face appeared above his—the man who came for him in New Orleans the other night, and who was waiting in his bathroom—and a fist clutched a pistol the wrong way around.

"Hold still," the man said, and Gardner covered his face, closing his eyes as the butt of the weapon struck his head.

He came to in a bar that seemed familiar and the last place he'd have expected to be, so he wondered if the afterlife didn't resemble the interior of the C'est La Vie: particleboard painted black, a video poker machine in the corner, and foil ashtrays on the tables. But was it heaven or hell? *I know which one I deserve.*

His head jerked. He licked his lips, tasting blood. That same Lauryn Hill song played on the stereo.

"I like to have killed him," a man said in a brogue—same guy who hit him with the pistol.

"Nah," said another man. "He's too hardheaded for that."

They laughed.

Gardner opened his eyes. The man with the mustache was sitting at the bar. Hayes—had to be. But how did they find Gardner, and what did they do with Krystal?

He tried to move his arms, but his wrists were fastened to the chair, his ankles tied with bailing twine. His cheek stung where the cane leaf cut it, and the side of his head ached where the man with the pistol hit him.

At the other end of the room, the man who chased him down in the cane field slurped noodles from a Happy Garden takeout container. A closed sign hung in the window, and the lights over the door were dark. No one else was in the place.

"We told management we were friends of yours," the man with the noodles said when Gardner stirred.

The man with the mustache laughed. "We are his friends. He just doesn't know it yet."

"Might be the only friends you have left in the world," the other man said through a mouthful of noodles.

"I'm listed," said the man with the mustache. "All your girl had to do was dial directory assistance to find me."

Gardner wasn't even surprised. Probably came back to find him gone and called from the payphone outside the bar. Or she got to thinking about how he roughed her up that morning, and didn't like that. Served him right.

The man with the mustache crossed the room, squatted in front of Gardner, and lifted his head. "Do you understand what's happening? You killed a man who worked for me. Ordinarily, you'd be floating in the gulf."

"You Hayes?" Gardner asked.

The guy seemed less impressive in person: a big dude, but nothing more.

"I'm Hayes," Leon Hayes said. "You've heard about me." He killed dozens, ordered the executions of dozens more, and was connected to both sides of the law up and down the Mississippi—all of that was true, and worse, he told Gardner.

But he was also a family man, he said.

"The man you killed was a piece of shit," Hayes said, "and he was pimping my niece, so I'm inclined to be lenient. You work for me now."

Hayes let go of Gardner's head. "You can think about it, if you need time. You know your options."

It surprised Gardner how easy the decision was to make. Must be why Hayes missed when he fired at Gardner in the doorway:

now that Gardner proved himself a killer, Hayes wanted to put him to work. Gardner felt elevated, or maybe this was what he wanted all along: power, the sense someone might be afraid of him, for a change.

His pants were still damp, and he smelled himself; the piss, the sour odor of fear. Recalling how he'd given up by the canal, his humiliation, he gritted his teeth. He wanted a chance to prove he wasn't a coward.

Maybe that was what redemption looked like: doubling down on your sins.

Hayes was halfway to the bar. Gardner said, "Fine."

He could become what the man wanted him to be: a killer, without remorse.

Without looking back, Leon nodded. "Cut him loose," he told the other man.

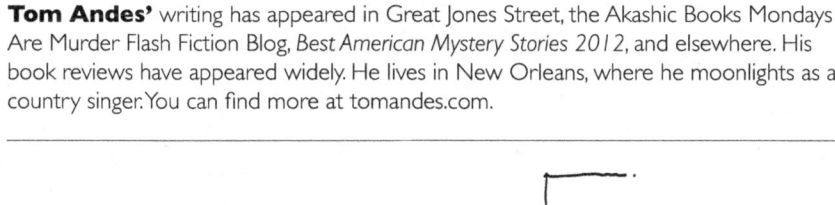

Tom Andes' writing has appeared in Great Jones Street, the Akashic Books Mondays Are Murder Flash Fiction Blog, *Best American Mystery Stories 2012*, and elsewhere. His book reviews have appeared widely. He lives in New Orleans, where he moonlights as a country singer. You can find more at tomandes.com.

© Tom Andes

"He's been shot 120 times. Let the coroner take him and do an autopsy to determine the cause of death."

Can we expect law and order in a society where justice is a relative issue?

Eleven Irritated People
by Preston Lang

You have to show photo ID to get on an airplane or into an elementary school. Bic needed ID at his grandma's nursing home so he could hear all about some poorly-cooked ham. Hell,

he even had to show ID the last time he saw an R-rated movie. But they don't check ID in the New York County Criminal Court building. Not on the way in and not when you raise your hand during attendance in the jury pool. There's never a moment in the whole process when they verify who you really are. It's possible they check ID for high-profile trials—murders and celebrity DUIs. But some kid looking at his third felony drug conviction? Come right on in, whoever you are. Who would be crazy enough to sneak into jury duty?

From the box, Bic watched the defendant walk in: Leonard James grimly followed a public defender in a bad suit.

Actually it wasn't even a suit, just a cheap-ass blazer with khakis and a four-dollar tie. Lennie kept his head down, and the judge did her song about Truth, Justice, and Reasonable Doubt. It wasn't until he'd pled not guilty that Lennie glanced at the jury for the first time. That's when he saw Bic and his eyes nearly fell out of his face. Bic gave his brother the slightest nod, and Lennie didn't look to the box again for the rest of the trial. One of the few smart moves he ever made in his life.

Not that it had been easy to get on Lennie's jury. When the trial date came around, Bic flew back to New York, put on his second-best suit, and walked into the courthouse on Centre Street then upstairs to the waiting room. He had a pretty good idea of the time Lennie's case was likely to come up. When they starting calling a morning panel, he waited for a no-response on a man's name. Henry Davis. Once, twice. When they called it a third and final time, Bic's hand shot up.

"Sorry, yeah. That's me."

But it was the wrong case. A man had robbed a liquor store with a metal pipe. Broke three of the owner's ribs over forty dollars. Bic got out of that one quick.

"My parents owned a liquor store. Like Mr. Bajaj, they were immigrants and were frequently the targets of—"

"Yes, thank you. You're excused."

Back into the pool. For the next panel, Bic had a bit of a problem. If they didn't call Henry Davis, should he respond as someone else? The lady upfront didn't seem to be paying attention to much of anything, but he'd already made himself a little memorable by waiting for three calls on the last panel. No, he had to stick with Henry Davis. If Henry didn't get called— Lennie was on his own.

The clerk droned out her selections, and people shuffled into the hall.

"Daniel Dowd? Daniel? Daniel Dowd? Last chance for Daniel Dowd."

Bic's hand almost went up, but—no—she'd had her coffee. She was looking more alert.

"Fine, no Daniel Dowd. How about Henry David? Sorry, Henry *Davis*?"

Henry Davis might have been some 60-year-old CEO who laughed at his jury summons or a 19-year-old hustler who did the exact same thing. Bic played him as a professional— midtown voice that was all business and just a little bit nerdy. During voire dire he said he was a chemical engineer who consulted for petroleum companies. There's plenty of racist bastards down on Centre Street, but it's not like a smart, Black guy in a nice suit is some kind of Yeti. No one doubted he was a successful engineer, but the prosecutor did ask just a few more questions than he'd asked some of the others. Yes, Bic could be impartial. Yes, he believed criminals should be punished. No, he did not feel the police were out to get young men of color.

The whole thing didn't take that long—four days testimony. They had Lenny cold. Witnesses, evidence, video of a cop pulling the bags out of Lennie's pocket. The prosecutor was a young guy—agile, animated, and very smug. And he had every right to be. He'd done his homework, and the guy from Legal Aid Society stammered and sweated and embarrassed himself on cross. The judge started to get impatient and hostile toward him, and a few times the jury laughed out loud when she rolled her eyes at one of his objections—*Counsellor, you can't object to the stenographer's hay fever.* But he did one thing right: he didn't put Lennie on the stand.

The trial wrapped up by 10:30 on a Friday, and eleven decent citizens were hoping to get back to their lives by lunchtime. A few unanimous votes and they'd all be on their way. The foreman, a bald Puerto Rican guy around 50, called for a vote right away. Possession with intent.

"All for guilty?" he asked.

Eleven hands went up right away. Then eleven sets of eyes shot to Henry Davis.

"I don't know if he's guilty."

Some of them thought it was a joke.

"I get it—if we stay until noon we all get a box lunch."

"I'm not convinced," Bic said.

"You saw the video, right?" the foreman said. "They took out the bags. Then they showed us those bags in evidence."

"How do we know they were the same bags?"

"You honestly think the police would pull something like that?"

"I have reasonable doubt, yes. Don't you?"

"No. No, I don't. I'm certain this guy is a drug dealer. What about the witnesses?"

"They were all criminals, right? That's what they told us."

"So this guy—Sweet Leonard—all around him it's dealers and punks, you think he's some kind of angel?"

"I'm saying that I have reasonable doubt. The judge told us that's all we need to vote not guilty."

A well-dressed white lady backed up the foreman.

"Come the hell on. His own lawyer thinks he's guilty. You can tell."

"I've met a lot of lawyers in my life," Bic said, "and that was the worst one I've ever seen."

"Fair point," the woman answered. "That doesn't make little Lennie innocent."

"I've got reasonable doubt even *with* the inadequate representation," Bic said. "What does that tell you?"

"I don't know—that Leonard promised you a kidney."

Another juror scoffed.

"Come on. The guy did it. Let's not play games. I'm already a week behind at work."

"In good conscience, I cannot send this man to prison."

Bic got roughed up from all sides for about an hour until a young white woman with a lot of homemade jewelry spoke for the first time.

"I think I vote not guilty, too."

"For Christ sake," the foreman said.

"The way we just railroad young Black men into the system—"

"Oh, for Christ sake," the foreman said—louder this time, shaking his head.

For a while it was just Henry Davis and his trusty, art-school sidekick.

"The more I think about it, the more I think of how laws are used against a kid like this," she said. "I think in a very real sense Leonard is innocent."

"But in another, much *more* real sense on Planet Earth, he is obviously guilty," the well-dressed lady said. "Do you hear that up there in your little spaceship?"

"Ma'am, please don't be disrespectful toward other jurors," Bic said.

She rolled her eyes.

"Okay, let's say you two really think some great wrong is being perpetrated here. It's not, but let's pretend it is. So here's the thing: we're only allowed to decide, based on the evidence, whether we think Leonard broke the laws as they currently stand. We are not allowed to make larger judgments just because we feel some higher calling."

"That's where you're wrong," Bic said. "We are allowed to find a defendant not guilty if we feel the law, or the process, or the society is unjust. We can—"

"Come off it."

"I will come off nothing. This is an established legal practice called jury-nullification. They don't like to tell you about it, but we have the option—no, we have the duty to go beyond the law when we feel it is necessary. The entire reason that twelve ordinary people like us are left to decide what happens to a fellow citizen is because *we* define justice. We are society."

"Jesus Christ. Listen to you."

"Yes, I hope we are all listening to each other."

The well-dressed woman started humming *We Shall Overcome*, but she didn't seem to get the laugh she was hoping for. Not too long after that, an older Black lady came over and a young Asian guy followed. Still eight-four in favor of conviction, but trending in the right direction. Then a heavy metal-looking dude with tattoos on his forearms piped up. Bic had him pegged for trouble from the start, but he was a pleasant surprise.

"Like Dr. Davis says—how do we know the bags they showed us were the same ones they took out of his pockets?"

Yeah, trust Henry Davis, Ph.D., chemical engineer, all-around good guy. But the foreman, the well-dressed lady, and the other solid citizens put up a fight.

"Where I grew up, a kid couldn't walk down the street," the foreman said. "I know who this Leonard is. He's got to be locked away, or he'll be back out there, getting kids high. And I

understand there's problems with the system. I hear that loud
and clear. But I cannot see any way that letting this guy go free
makes anything better for anyone."

They brought in food. The jurors were antsy: there were no
vegetarian sandwiches, and the meat was too salty. When the
meal was over they went around in circles for another two
hours. Then one of the decent citizens came over—*I have to get
back to work. What was one more dealer on the streets?* That
quickly opened the door to three more defections.

"You guys are not taking this seriously," the foreman said.
"We have to be serious."

But when he saw he wasn't bringing anyone back, he sent a
message to the judge—they wouldn't be able to reach a decision.
Bic was going to object, but he knew the judge wouldn't accept
a mistrial at this point. Not so soon. And he was right. The judge
told them to keep at it. She probably thought there was a lone
holdout for not guilty, and more time would bring that nut
around. She didn't realize it was going the other way.

Night came and the holdouts started to fall. Two of them
buckled together just after midnight. It took another hour
to break the well-dressed woman. She went down with an
ugly, fake laugh—*Forgive me, oh Themis.* Finally at three in the
morning, the foreman started to waver.

"You just don't care about what's right and what's wrong.
None of you."

He owned two bakeries in Inwood. He had three children and
four grandkids. His wife had early onset dementia. Clearly a
decent guy—not quite a moral superhero.

"Fine. He's innocent. He should get a prize. I'm going to track
him down and give him a God damn pineapple cake. Maybe
ask him to look after my grandson while my daughter is at
night school. What a fantastic dude. Not Guilty. Not Guilty. Not
Guilty."

They trudged back into the courtroom and gave the verdict.
The judge was silent for a moment. Obviously she knew things
had gotten strange in the jury room, but she hadn't considered
the possibility that twelve reasonably competent adults could
find Leonard not guilty. For a second she stared at the box like

it was full of live rats. Then she spat out a *thanks for your service* and let Lennie go free.

The not-guilty party was probably a lot of fun, or maybe Lennie took a switchblade to everyone he thought had snitched. Either way, Bic wasn't going anywhere near it. He was on a plane back to California five hours after the verdict was read. He waited until the next day to call.

"Man, how did you do that? I mean, what did you—"

"Shut up. Just don't talk at all," Bic said. "This is it, Len. You're on your own."

"Yeah, no. I see. I see how it is. The only reason I even got—"

"Shut up. Just shut up. Maybe you want to do something else. Maybe not. I don't know. It's your life, but I can't help you anymore."

Bic hung up on his brother. Half-brother. In his mind he could hear Lennie talking to friends: my brother knows everything, can talk his way out of anything, snuck his way onto my jury. And then Bic could hear him telling all that to a DA the next time he got arrested.

Three-and-a-half weeks later, a Washington Heights busboy received a check in the mail for 113 dollars from the New York State Supreme Court. He remembered getting the summons about a month back, but he'd ignored it because he knew if he took a few days off, the restaurant would find someone else who knew how to use a napkin. He considered the possibility that the check was a trap, a sting to catch jury truants, but finally he decided that 113 bucks was worth the risk. He cashed it at Pay-O-Matic and then bought his girlfriend a thin chain with a dangling, golden letter H for Honoria. After that, Henry Davis never looked back.

Preston Lang currently lives New York with his wife and daughter. He's published three crime novels to date with a few more to come out in 2018. He's thrilled to be back at *Pulp Modern*. For more check out prestonlangbooks.com

Stubborn might as well be a synonym for stupid.

Second Chances
by John Teel

Josh was pacing back and forth in the cold when Scott pulled into the parking lot of Fathead's Bar. Josh whipped the door open and hurried inside, slamming it hard behind him. Scott shot him an irritated glance.

"Sorry," Josh said between blowing into his cupped hands. "I've been waiting a while. Where you been?"

Scott got the car moving and said, "I had a meeting with Mr. Darby."

Josh stopped blowing hot air and stared at Scott.

"A meeting?" he asked. "About what? Who else was there?"

Scott shrugged. "A couple of the guys. No big deal."

"No big deal? Why didn't anybody tell me about it? How many's a couple?" Josh sat up straight as a light pole.

"Me. Sam. Vinny and Mark. The usual suspects."

Scott piloted the car off the Boulevard and onto the turnpike. They drove in silence.

Finally, Josh spoke. "Nobody bothered to call me?"

Scott was silent.

"What was the meeting about, Scott?"

Scott didn't answer. He just sighed.

"It was about me wasn't it?"

Scott took the second exit off the turnpike and continued down some back roads, popping out where the trees lined either side of the road, the darkness hiding anything amongst their ranks. Josh looked out the window and realized where they were headed. He also realized his pistol was nestled under his mattress at home instead of on his hip. Stupid. He should've known he was in trouble. He just never would've guessed they'd send Scott to do their dirty work.

"How long have we known each other?" Josh asked, trying to play the friendship card and buy himself a little time.

"Since grade school."

"That's right, since grade school. And this is how you're gonna' do me? Take me out to Darby's acres and whack me out. Is that it? Is that what your little pow-wow was about tonight?" Josh's heart was pounding his chest like a woodpecker on speed.

Scott's silence gave him his answer.

"This is about the bookie," Josh said shaking his head. "I knew it. I fucking knew it."

"You were supposed to scare the guy, not kill him. What did you expect?" There was a sadness in Scott's voice. It gave Josh a tiny cunt hair of hope.

"It was your idea to hang him over the side of the building, not mine."

"Yeah and it would've worked out fine, but you dropped him."

Josh waved his hands. "Technically his shoe slipped off and I lost my grip."

"Technically, you dropped him," Scott said.

"How pissed was he?" Josh was going to keep him talking as much as possible.

Scott shrugged. "The guy made Darby a lot of money. You know how long Darby's been skimming him. The envelopes started getting light. We were supposed to remind him why he should be respectful of Mr. Darby and to remember his place in all of this. Instead, he ended up with his head cracked open and his brain on the outside of his body. Mr. Darby took a pretty big hit to his pocket with that little fuck up and it ain't like this is the first fuck up there's been with you. I'd say he was pretty pissed."

"Shit."

"Yeah. Shit."

Scott hung a left through the trees onto a rocky, unpaved road, the trees so close the branches slapped the windshield and scraped against the sides of the car. No Trespassing signs were nailed to the old, oak trunks every twenty feet. The road was blocked by a tall, wrought iron gate. Scott rolled his window down to punch the code into the number pad. Josh noticed the pistol in his other hand. He knew what was beyond the gate. This was where they brought people to disappear. It was where you went when Darby wanted you gone. He wished he had come here under better circumstances.

"Scott. Wait."

Scott sighed again. His face was drained of color and his hand shook ever so slightly. Josh couldn't remember ever seeing Scott look so tired. "It's gotta' be done. If I don't do this, it'll be both of us dead. You know how he is."

Josh's brain was scrambling. This was it. But he could sense a hesitation in Scott's voice.

"I can disappear. You know I can. What have I got here anyway? My parents are dead. My brother's a shit stain. I haven't talked to him in years. No kids. No girlfriend. No friends, besides you." Josh tried his best to turn on the water works, but it wasn't happening. The best he could do was to make a really sad face and mock whimper. It seemed to be working. "I don't wanna' die, Scott. I fucked up, I know it. I accept it, ok? But you're gonna' kill me? For him? Really?"

Scott was looking at his lap, the gun in his hand resting on his thigh.

"At least look at me before you kill me," Josh said.

Scott holstered his pistol and held Josh's gaze. "Fuck him," Scott said.

Josh exhaled a shaky breath and then the dams finally burst. He just couldn't help himself. It felt good to be alive.

After backing out the way they came and finding the main road, Scott drove them to a bar off the beaten path. They sat and ordered beers from a man who looked about one more bad day away from swallowing a buckshot sandwich. The beer was skunked and tasted like a bottled fart, but Josh thought it was the best thing that'd ever passed his lips. The color was back in Scott's face. He took a long drink from his bottle and then ordered two shots of whiskey. The bartender was not happy about it.

"What're we doing here?" Josh asked.

"We're celebrating."

"Celebrating what?"

"Your life, my friend." Scott smiled as the shots were slammed down in front of them. Scott picked one up and placed it in front of Josh. He raised it. "To second chances." They clinked glasses and swallowed the piss warm liquor.

"Keep them coming bartender," Scott said. The bartender slammed the bottle down in front of them and made no further contact the rest of the night.

"I gotta' watch myself with whiskey," Josh said as Scott poured him another. "You remember how crazy I used to get?"

Scott chuckled. "I remember you passing out a lot and the rest of us messing with you while you slept. And if I remember correctly, it wasn't just whiskey. It was everything. I have about ten years worth of pictures of you in compromising positions. I could've butt-fucked you and you would've woke up thinking Budweiser gave you anal cramps."

Josh smiled. "That's my super power. I can sleep through anything."

"I wish your super power was not dropping guys off of buildings. Then maybe we wouldn't be in this predicament."

"Come on," Josh said. "Let's not talk about that. Why're you bringing up old shit?"

"All right, after this I promise, no more talking about it. But you have to listen to me. When we leave here, you're gonna' grab some stuff from your house. Quickly. Then you're in an Uber and you're gone. And I mean gone, Josh. You go to the airport and get a ticket. Somewhere on the west coast. Somewhere he isn't connected. Go to California, man. Relax for a while. I know you have some dough saved up."

"I got a little stash," Josh said with a grin.

"Good. Once you go you can never come back. I'll tell him you were gone when I went to your house. I'll tell him you've been acting jumpy since the accident with the bookie. I think I can sell it to him."

"That fucking bookie," Josh said shaking his head. He slammed back his shot and quickly poured another. "I gotta' piss." He walked to the bathroom as if the room was on a slant.

Scott pulled the burner phone from his pocket and checked it. One message from Darby.

Is it done?

"Son of a bitch," Scott grumbled, stuffing the phone back in his pocket. He walked over to the jukebox and got a few classic rock tunes blaring. Josh danced his way back from the bathroom and together they slammed back shot after shot at the bar. By the third song the bartender pulled the plug on the jukebox and then locked himself in the bathroom. He never came back out.

Scott drove out of there along the backroads with one eye open, trying his best to maintain a safe speed and keep the swerving down to a minimum. Meanwhile, Josh had his dick hanging out of the window, a stream of piss blowing into the passenger door and the back window.

"Jesus Christ, man. You're hosing that off when we get to your house."

"Nope," Josh said, "Gotta' get going. You told me I gotta' disappear as quickly as possible. Aint' got the time for all that." Josh stuck his head out the window and screamed like a drunk chick in a limo ride at her bachelorette party.

"Low profile, dickhead," Scott said, rolling the window up.

"Fuck that. Fuck Darby. We should go and deal with him Scotty. He tried to pit us against each other. He treats us like we're fucking dopes. We could do just as good a job as he does. We could whack him out and take that whole rinky dink operation over."

Scott opened his other eye and took a long look at Josh. "You're right about one thing," he said. "You do have to watch yourself with whiskey. It makes you fucking retarded."

"I'm not joking Scott. It'd be easy to take him out."

Scott pulled the car over to the shoulder, the tires kicking up gravel and dust, and killed the lights. "Shut your fucking mouth. You're my friend, and I love you, but if you suggest some stupid ass shit like that again I just might change my mind. There's nothing else for you here. Get that revenge shit out of your head. It's over. You get me?"

Josh grunted as he slumped down in his seat.

Scott smacked him hard in the shoulder. "Do you get me?"

"Yeah, yeah, yeah I fucking get you." Josh crossed his arms in a huff.

"Good." Scott flicked the lights back on and they drove in silence. Once they reached the turnpike, Josh got to yawning, sinking lower and lower into his seat. Then he began to laugh, a low, drunken giggle that built and built until his body shook like a chilly, tourettes patient. Scott laughed too at how ridiculous he looked. "You are fucked up," Scott said.

"That I am."

The laughter grew and grew. Something about it was making Scott uncomfortable.

"What's so funny?" Scott asked.

Josh could barely contain himself and between guffaws he managed to sputter out a sentence. "I swear I didn't drop that bookie on purpose. But the irony is, we were sending a message because his envelopes were light. And I was the one lightening them." He howled with laughter, holding his belly and doubling over in his seat. Scott's mouth hung open like a prostitute with lockjaw. "Where do you think I got most of my stash? Darby, that cheap prick, he's got enough money. Pays us peanuts to do his dirty work. Well I got me a little extra compensation on the side. And when we get to the house I'm gonna' reward you handsomely my friend. Even though you thought about taking my ass out, you came to your senses. You've always been loyal."

"You're serious?" Scott asked.

"Duh," Josh said, followed by more laughter.

"You fucking idiot," Scott said.

"Don't be mad. It's over, remember? A couple years from now, Darby won't even remember this shit." He hiccuped and yawned again, long and loud. "I'll straighten things out with him later."

There it was again. Scott knew once Josh had something in his head it was staying there until he got it out. He wasn't going to let it go, which meant the blowback would be on Scott. Scott eased off the turnpike and took the boulevard the rest of the way. Next to him Josh's mouth was open wide, a noise like a table saw buzzing from the back of his throat. Scott checked his burner again. Another message from Darby.

Call me.

"Fuck off," Scott said, tossing the phone into the back seat.

He turned off the boulevard and coasted down Josh's street, the giant oak trees shading the street from the fat, ripe moon above. Scott gave Josh a nudge. "Wake up."

Josh snorted and he smacked his lips like he'd just eaten a spoonful of peanut butter, but his eyes didn't open. Scott gave him a rougher shove and his head just rolled to one side, the snoring louder than ever now. Scott was hit with a sudden wave of deja vu of the time in high school when Josh had passed out after drinking all night and he and three of their buddies posed him with different items around the house and took pictures of it all.

A toothbrush in one hand, toothpaste in the other.

A bowl with two eggs in it and an eggbeater placed in his grip.

Scissors in his left hand, a sheet of coupons in his right.

At first the guys were gentle with Josh's limbs, gingerly posing his hands and arms and suppressing their laughter so as not to wake him. After a while they realized there was no waking him. He was almost comatose. His eyes never fluttered. His lips never trembled. He was dead to the world. For an hour they roughly moved his body into different positions and took pictures; laughing, shouting and drinking.

Scott surveyed the street, but nothing moved. He reached across and patted Josh's pockets finding his keys and pulling them out with no great effort, the jingling unusually loud in the quiet car. Scott walked up the driveway to Josh's garage door and gripped the handle, turning it right and lifting the door overhead. Josh's beat up Chevy sat there like a rusty sarcophagus. He looked back at Josh drooling on himself in his car. His friend.

"Goddamn you," he whispered.

Scott opened the passenger side door and gripped Josh under both armpits. He pulled him out, his feet smacking the pavement, and drug him up the driveway; his heels scraping the ground sounded like a rake on a chalkboard, but Josh still did not stir. In the garage, Scott unlocked the driver's side door and heaved Josh in. He put the keys in the ignition and hesitated, the guilt swirling in his chest like a storm front.

"Gonna' get his," Josh mumbled and then his jaw hung slack, the snoring starting again.

Scott shook his head and turned the key, the engine roaring to life. He wiped everything down he had touched and closed the door. He walked back to the overhead door. He watched as exhaust belched from the tailpipe. Josh's head never moved an inch.

He really can sleep through anything.

A sad smile drew at the corner of Scott's mouth as he closed the garage up, wiping the handle down when he was through. Scott got back in his car and found his burner lying on the floor in the back. He flipped it open and texted Darby.

It's done.

He snapped the phone in two and stuffed it under his seat; safe keeping for its eventual disposal. Starting the car, he imagined Josh gulping in the fumes, his breath shallow until eventually, his body shut down. No more breaths. No more bad decisions. Josh gave him no choice. He tried to let him go. As always, Josh got in his own way. It beat the alternative;

dismemberment, most of his body fed to Darby's pigs, the rest burned and scattered like so much dust in the breeze.

It's for the best, Scott told himself.

He took a long look at the garage, a part of him expecting the door to open and Josh to emerge, a drunken smile on his face. If there was anyone who could fuck up dying it was surely him. But the door never opened. He never emerged. He slept and he wouldn't wake up. Scott sighed.

It was never easy being his friend.

He shifted into drive and headed towards home.

John Teel is a union ironworker from Philly. His work can be found in *Shotgun Honey, Dark Moon Digest, The Literary Hatchet* and *Out of the Gutter.* When he isn't working he's spending time with his kids and the ugliest rescue dog you've ever laid eyes on.

© John Teel

SOLDAN
McQUISTON
RUTHERFORD
MANZOLILLO
HEIJNDERMANS
GRAVES
GRAY
PLATT
PERRY
HIVNER
TURNER III

ECONO CLASH review
ONE

QUALiTY CHEAP THRiLLS

ECONOCLASHREVIEW.BLOGSPOT.COM

Vengeance is always divine work.

Sacrifice
by Robert Petyo

When I received the certified letter telling me my insurance claim had been denied and that I was responsible for all the charges, I decided that somebody had to die. The angry gods were screwing me, and the only way to appease them was with a sacrifice. My daddy used to tell me that whenever things went wrong, the gods were angry. That's why there were wars in the world, he said. That's why he couldn't keep a good job. That's why it rained on his wedding day. Angry gods.

And when the gods were angry, you had to appease them with a sacrifice.

Clearly, the gods were angry with me. I didn't know why, but they were. In the last three months, nothing had gone right. The Magistrate wouldn't listen to me about the speeding ticket. My insurance was going to go up and I could barely afford the payments now. Without a car, I'd be screwed. I was on probation at work because of my fight with Cashman. One more misstep and I'd be fired. I had struggled long and hard on that job, slaving away on the night shift for years before finally getting reasonable hours. The pay wasn't great, but it kept me going. And now my wife was starting to moan about never having gone on a nice, expensive vacation.

I needed a sacrifice.

Then things would turn around for me.

Whether it was my insurance man Sincavage who had first lured me to United, or the policeman who had

filed the report indicating that Jamie was driving, or Jamie who did not tell me that he had lost his license two months before, or my worthless cousin Marjoe who was driving the other car and insisted on calling the police after a minor fender bender, or my wife who had demanded that I give Jamie a chance to make something of himself, or even the stupid mailman who delivered the goddamn letter, it didn't matter. Somebody had to be sacrificed.

Jamie would be the easiest to kill. Lord knows, he deserved it. He was a jobless slug who was costing me a fortune. But suspicion would immediately fall on me, just as it would if I sacrificed my nagging wife, Sally. I was too close to them. I wanted to make the necessary sacrifice, but I didn't want to end up in jail. Daddy had spent time in jail and it hadn't done him any good.

Marjoe was a problem, too. That we despised each other was well known in our respective families. If she were sacrificed, I would be an immediate suspect.

Sincavage was a possibility. Let's face it. Everybody hates insurance salesmen.

The cop would have lots of potential enemies, too. Plenty of suspects. But killing a cop was risky. They'd spare no expense investigating that one.

No. My best chance for a safe human sacrifice would be to kill the mailman. It would appear to be one of those seemingly random acts of violence that fill our society nowadays. No one would suspect me. The sacrifice would be made. The gods would be appeased. My wife would stop nagging me. The insurance company would reconsider. I'd get a raise at work.

I arranged to skip work on Thursday. I told Sally I wasn't feeling well. She displayed a little concern before hustling off to that cheap downtown diner where she worked breakfast and lunch. I guess I should appreciate the fact that she was trying to help out, but the few bucks that waitressing brought in didn't seem to be worth her time. And I think she enjoyed flirting with the customers instead of handling more important chores around the house.

I waited near the window in our front room around eleven

o'clock, which was usually when the mailman showed up.

I wasn't going to do it here. I just wanted to talk to him and arrange to meet somewhere, maybe a dark parking lot where I could make it look like a mugging gone bad.

It was closer to noon when he finally showed up and I yanked the door open, startling him so that he fumbled his handful of letters. "You're not my regular mailman," I said, trying not to shout.

He backed away and crouched to pick up the two letters he had dropped. "I'm new on the route," he said as he straightened and shifted his satchel slightly so that it shielded him.

"Where's my regular guy?"

"He bid to a different route. Started it today."

"Tom was his name, right?"

"No. Hank. Hank Burnside."

"Oh yeah. I got mixed up. Tom works at the store down the street."

He handed me my mail and waited.

"I just wanted to thank him for—" What could I say? I had to make my curiosity seem natural. If, after the fact, this man recalled my questions, suspicion would fall on me. I had to cover my tracks. Daddy always said you had to carefully think things through. "I wanted to thank him for helping me out the other day when I couldn't get my car started."

"Sure. Hank's a good guy."

"Yeah."

After a few seconds of silence, the mailman turned and shuffled off.

I ducked back inside and turned on the computer. I clapped my hands as if that would speed it up, and I took a few deep breaths to calm myself as it booted. The gods were testing me by throwing obstacles in my path. But when I persevered and passed each test, the result would be even sweeter. The gods would appreciate all I went through to appease them.

When I accessed an on-line directory, I found three Burnsides listed. None was a Henry or a Hank, but there was one on Filbert Street, less than a half mile from my house. I took that as a good omen.

That evening, while Sally overcooked spaghetti noodles, I called.

"Hank's not here right now," a man said.

Jackpot! "We've been out of touch for a while," I said, hoping to sound like an old friend looking him up. "Do you know where he is?"

"This time of day, he's probably at Hanratty's. He usually stops there after work."

Further proof the gods were finally willing to allow my sacrifice. Hanratty's was a secluded bar with a poorly lit parking lot. I went there often when I had life sorrows to drown.

The next day was Friday, a bar night. Sally went to a movie with her sister, so I took a pocketknife from my cluttered garage workshop and went to Hanratty's. The bar was dim, crowded and noisy. I didn't see Burnside, but I couldn't be positive that he wasn't there amongst the crowd that shuffled about, slapping each other on the back and clinking glasses. I could wait. I sat at the rectangular bar that was surrounded by round tables scattered like discarded checkers and ordered a beer.

After my third one, I got up to go to the men's room.

"Is that you, Albert?"

I tensed and slipped one hand into my pocket where the knife was snug against my thigh.

"Albert?" I felt a hand on my shoulder and had to turn. It was Burt Cashman, a burly man with fields of black hair on the backs of his hands. He was a foreman at the plant. "What the heck are you doing here?"

I shrugged and tilted my head toward my empty glass. "The wife's gone out with her sister. I thought I'd stop for a few."

He smiled and tried to elbow me, but missed. "Great idea. Celebrate a night of freedom. Want some company?"

"No." I said it too quickly and too loudly. I didn't want his company. I wanted to hit him. Cashman was toeing the company line and trying to reconcile things between us by buddying up to me. But I wanted to stay as far from him as possible.

Now his hooded, shaggy brows showed his feelings were hurt. He would remember this encounter. I was no longer a faceless drinker in the crowd. There was no chance of my making the sacrifice tonight, even if I could find Burnside. I would have to wait for another day. "I think I better be heading back," I said.

He burped and staggered away.

I turned and bumped into Hank Burnside.

"Excuse me," he said as he shifted to allow me to pass.

I kept my head down.

"Mr. Kniffen?" He tapped two fingertips against my clavicle.

I wanted to flee.

"Don't you know me?" he asked.

I pretended to scrutinize him in the dimness. "My mailman, aren't you?"

"I was. I just bid to a different route."

"Oh. Why?"

"Well, I—" He stopped and turned toward the bar. "Have a drink with me."

I stepped away.

"Come on. I'll buy."

"Just let me hit the head. I'll be right back."

"What are you drinking?"

I told him to order me a Bud and hurried to the men's room. I thought about walking out and leaving him at the bar. But then he would remember this encounter and might tell his friends at work. A connection would be made between us. On the other hand, if I spent some time with him, gathered some information, another opportunity might present itself. I might come up with a better plan.

Daddy always said that the gods worked in mysterious ways.

"You look beat," I said when I returned.

"It's work." He raised his glass to his lips, hesitated, and set it back down without drinking. "Anderson," he said with obvious distaste.

"Who's that? Your boss?" I slipped onto the stool beside him.

"Nah. My union steward. He's a useless piece of shit. I'm getting screwed out of overtime and I can't get him to back me. He won't file a grievance."

"He has to, doesn't he? It's his job as a steward, right?"

"He says I don't have a gripe."

"Then get yourself a new steward."

"It ain't that easy."

"I used to be one," I said. It was leftover tensions from my union activist days that led to my problems with Cashman. "It was my job to fight for the workers, no matter what I thought about them being right or wrong. That part wasn't my call."

He turned and patted my shoulder. "Buddy, we could use a few fighters like you down at the Post Office."

I took a long sip of my beer. I felt relaxed, at ease. How many drinks was this? Two was usually my limit. "So how are they screwing you, Hank?"

He told me a long story about route inspections, penalty overtime, pivoting, and non-reportable accidents. I understood none of it, but I could see that Hank Burnside was not a happy man.

"The stress is getting to me," he said. "It's why I spend so much time here."

"It sounds to me like Anderson isn't your problem."

"No?"

"The boss O'Mara is the guy causing all your troubles. He does the scheduling. He writes the discipline."

"You got that right," he said after another sip of beer. "He is a prick. So what do I do about it?"

"My daddy used to say that if you're having some problems, then the gods must be angry."

He chuckled. "So what do I do about angry gods?"

"A sacrifice usually does the trick."

"You mean like penance? Should I give up beer for a week or something like that?"

I grinned. "I was thinking about something a little more direct."

"Such as?"

"Well, O'Mara's your problem, so make him the sacrifice."

"How?"

"Kill him."

His glass made a hollow boom as he thumped it on the bar. He didn't look at me and he didn't laugh or act shocked. He simply gazed across the bar as he considered what I said.

"Think about it. You admit he's a prick. If he's gone, so's

your problem."

"Nah," he finally said, lifting his beer again. "The next guy would be just as bad. It's like they have an assembly line of managers, each one a bigger prick than the one before. You'd have to kill them all." He turned to me, his eyes slightly milky. "That ain't gonna happen. I could do O'Mara. Believe me, I could. Get me mad enough, and I could do it. But the next one. And the next one. No way. It'd never work," he said with a sigh. "How about you? Could you do it?"

"I think so."

"Good for you." He pointed at my glass. "Another one?"

"Thanks, but no thanks." I slid off the stool. "It's time to call it a night."

"Will I see you again here sometime?"

"Probably."

"You're a good guy, Mr. Kniffen."

"Call me Al."

"Okay, Al. I like you. You're easy to talk to." He turned back to the bar and grabbed his glass as I waved and walked away.

Sally was waiting when I got home. "Where have you been?"

I could tell right away she was in the mood for a fight. She loved fights. They revived her after a long day. But I had other things on my mind, so I ignored her and headed for the stairs.

"Albert."

She only called me Albert on fight nights.

She caught my arm as I tried to slip past her. I swung and shoved her away. She went down in front of the sofa, her legs sprawled out. Her eyes flared like flash bulbs as she glared at me. She looked frightened.

"Not tonight," I said. "I have a headache."

The next day I took an early lunch and went to the Post Office. It was about a mile from the plant. The lobby was a long rectangle divided into two sections by an open glass door. The first section, just off the parking lot was lined with post office boxes and small counters for patrons to prepare packages. The second section, the window lobby, had a long counter where customers were lined up and clerks sold stamps.

I rang the bell to my left to get access to the administrative offices, and a tinny voice came through a speaker under a pencil point video camera.

"Can I help you?"

"I'd like to speak to Tim O'Mara."

"Your name?"

"Alan Jones," I lied.

"Is he expecting you?"

I didn't like talking to people I couldn't see. "Just tell him to get out here." There was a window in the upper half of the door, but it was tinted so I could only see blurred images through it.

After several minutes, another voice came through the speaker. A man's voice rife with impatience. "Can I help you?"

"I want to talk to Tim O'Mara."

"What about?"

"Are you O'Mara?"

No response.

"Come out and face me man to man." Sounds from the lobby around me seemed to swell and I couldn't hear the man's response. I gazed up at the video camera. "I'm here about Hank Burnside."

"What about him?"

"Just get out here." I checked my watch. I still had about half an hour, but this guy's stalling was riling me.

The door opened and he bulled out. He was over six feet tall, stocky, with a walrus mustache that was flecked with gray. His eyes were hidden behind tinted wire rims.

"You O'Mara?"

"You Jones?"

"That's right."

"How do you know Hank Burnside?"

"My cousin."

"I see." He folded his arms and rocked on his heels. "What can I do for you?"

"I want you to stop harassing him."

"Excuse me?"

"Get off his back, or I'll have my lawyers down on you so fast you'll be buried so deep in lawsuits and paperwork that you won't see the sunshine."

"I think you misunderstand a few things."

"No." I jabbed a finger at him. "You misunderstand things. You can't keep getting away with this harassment. I want the disciplinary letters to stop. I want you to stop mistreating my cousin. You understand me?"

"I don't know who you are, or what you think you can accomplish by coming here, but you are way out of line." He raised his hand as if to slap me, but stiffened and raised his index finger, making his point. "We are finished here." He turned and punched a code into the keypad.

"You'll be hearing from my lawyers," I snapped as I spun and strode away.

I had no lawyers, and Burnside wasn't my cousin. I had no idea if what O'Mara was doing qualified as illegal harassment or not, but I did know that floor level supervisors in plants were often intimidated by the thought of labor lawyers getting involved.

And I did know that I finally started feeling a lot better.

I was turning to leave when I heard the scream from inside the window lobby behind me. I spun back toward the sound.

"He's got a gun." It was a woman's voice, high pitched and shredded with terror.

I started toward the glass door.

The crowd was fleeing, scattering toward me, some ducking through a second door onto Main Street, others looping around an outcropping wall of metal boxes to hide, others racing past me toward the exit to the parking lot.

But I ignored the flow and moved into the window lobby. I saw him as clearly as if we were only inches apart. He held a wailing woman's neck in the bend of his elbow. She was bent back over his thigh like a dying tree branch. The revolver he held was pointed up under her chin.

It was Burnside.

"Get O'Mara out here," he shouted to the clerks behind the counter. "Now." He saw me standing in the entranceway to the outer lobby. There was a moment of recognition, followed by a grim smile. "Stay back."

I turned and saw O'Mara coming out of the offices. With a wave of my arm I beckoned him.

He saw what was happening behind me and turned to flee toward the parking lot.

Sighing, I turned back to the gunman.

"Don't do it, Hank," somebody pleaded.

I saw that everyone in the window lobby had taken cover. Clerks cowered down behind the counter. There were no customers left. It was just me and Hank. And the terrified woman.

"Stay back," he shouted when I took a step forward. "Get O'Mara out here."

"He's gone," I said.

"Go get him."

"He's a coward," I said as I took another step forward. "He ran away." I pointed back toward the parking lot behind me. "What else would you expect from a scumbag like him?"

He made a sneering face and swung his arm out, dropping the woman like a sack of rocks.

I was moving before she hit the floor.

He had turned toward the counter, apparently planning to leap over it and charge into the innards of the post office, but he swung back toward me as I charged.

Too late.

I crashed into him and we soared across the floor, taking down a portable bulletin board filled with pictures of decorative stamps.

He grunted as I landed on top of him and we rolled on the floor. I twisted and drove my forearm into his jaw, knocking his head against the tile floor, but he managed to snake one arm behind my back, hugging me. With his other hand he tried to raise the gun but I pinned his forearm down with my wrist.

When Hank ripped his gun arm free from my grasp, I didn't hesitate. I slammed his head down on the tile floor. Hard. Twice. The second time, I heard something crack.

He went limp and his arms dropped to the floor. The gun clattered away with a hollow plastic sound.

Policemen arrived.

Sure, I thought. Now they show up.

But people were clapping as someone helped me to my feet.

"You saved me. Thank God. You saved me." It was the hostage. A pretty woman with short, red hair. I hadn't gotten a good look at her before. All I saw was the gun.

She hugged me.

Wow, I thought. I couldn't remember the last time anybody hugged me that tightly. Certainly not Sally.

A policeman, his gun drawn, was crouched near Hank's body. Blood pooled on the tile beneath Hank's head.

Another policeman stood near Hank's discarded gun, looking down at it, shaking his head. "Plastic," he said softly. "It's a toy." He looked up at me. "Don't worry, buddy. You're a hero."

I barely heard him. The people were still cheering, and the woman still hugged me as if she would die if she let go.

I realized the gods were smiling on me and my life was about to get a lot better.

Robert Petyo's crime stories have appeared in small press magazines and on the web, most recently at "Mystery Weekly," "Spinetingler," "Flash Bang Mysteries," "Yellow Mama" and in the anthologies *A Bit of a Twist*, and *Beautiful Lies, Painful Truths*.

He has also published some science fiction in small press magazines, and in the deep dark past he wrote three science fiction novels under three different names.

In his other life, he is happily married and has three grown children. He lives in northeastern Pennsylvania, is recently retired from the US Postal Service and enjoys playing with his adorable grandson. He can be reached at petyo@ptd.net.

© Robert Petyo

All business is crime.

Quick Cash Fast
by Charles Roland

The first time Simon Bridge brought a girl home, his dad gave him some real good advice.

That's what the old man called it when something crossed his mind to say to the boy. "Hey, Si," he'd say, with an arm over Simon's shoulder, "let me give you some real good advice."

Simon was fourteen. The girl was pretty and shy, waiting on the front steps.

This time the real good advice was: "Don't fuck her all at once, you know?"

Simon nodded like he knew, but inside his fourteen-year-old

head he was thinking: *How you want me to fuck her, then? A little at a time? Like, just the tip?*

But looking back now, more than twenty years later, Simon thought he knew what the old man meant.

You've got to take things slow. A little here, a little there. Bit by bit, not all at once. That's how you build. That's how you get somewhere.

They got the old man on some bullshit, and he ended up with life plus twenty up at Monroe-Keowah Regional Detention Center. Still, one thing you could say about Simon's dad, he knew some things.

Motherfucker was *smart*.

Simon was smart, too.

Driving to the scene, air going full blast in the July heat, Reg Colclough gazed blankly out the window, letting Monroe, South Carolina form an impression. This time of night, there weren't many other cars on Broad Street to worry about, and he knew the stoplights pretty well.

For what felt like the hundredth or thousandth time, he watched the signs flash past, and his distaste built.

EZ Cash

$$ Right Now

Cash for Gold

These businesses were closed for the day, heavy steel bars over their doors and windows. The fast food restaurants interspersed between them were still open.

Shit, he thought. *Which way you want to die?*

Bleed you broke, or feed you sick?

He knew that after his shift was over he'd stop back here for a drive-through breakfast, which he'd consume, heavy with resignation, on his drive out of the city and into the county, to the ranch home he shared with his wife and two children.

No Credit Check

Quick Cash Fast

$$$ Today

Colclough turned off of Broad Street, and the road got dark. A few more turns and he was at the scene, nestled within Monroe's hard-ass south side, where the murder rate made Colclough feel like he was big city police.

He stepped out of the car, and thought: *Why not kill each other?*

It would give those folks back on Broad Street some competition.

The idea came to Simon back in June, when he was dead broke. So broke, in fact, that he walked into a loan office—QUICK CASH FAST—and put up the title to his car for $500, which was money he'd split between his ex-wife, the landlord, the City of Monroe (who charged you $10 each week you were late on the water bill), the power company, and the gas station man who'd give you credit if you paid ten percent above in a week or so.

The car had been the old man's. Not that Simon liked it so much, but it hurt to sign it over for what felt like pocket change. Not nearly enough to get him back above water.

One thing you could say about being broke: It doesn't leave you with much in the way of pride.

Simon signed the papers and walked out with the loan officer's hand on his shoulder, into the big lot out front of the building all packed with cars. Old cars, new cars. Cars that looked all beat up, and cars that looked like someone had spit-shined them that morning.

All those cars, and there hadn't been but three or four people in the office.

Then Simon looked again, and caught the stickers on the windshields. Big, puffy numbers: $2,000; $2,500; $4,000.

The cars were for sale.

He turned to the loan officer.

"You sell cars?" he asked.

"Yep," said the man. He looked around, squinting in the sun. "Cars, trucks. Houses, even. What you looking for?"

Simon thought about that.

"Where'd you get them cars?" he asked, guessing the answer but wanting to hear it anyway.

The loan officer smiled, almost apologetically, and looked down at the loan paperwork Simon held folded up in his hand. Then the man shrugged.

That's when it clicked for Simon.

They don't want that $500 back, he thought.
They don't want the money.
They want the cars.

Colclough lit a cigarette before he went inside, leaning up against his car and looking at the patrol officers standing around the body, the men in boxer shorts on nearby porches, the women trying to keep their kids inside.

He'd started smoking when he'd moved back to Monroe. His wife called it "going native."

I'm from here, he wanted to say. *I am a native.*

Truth was, he liked smoking. He liked the time it gave him to think, the opportunity to stand somewhere, alone and quiet, listening to himself inhale and exhale.

His wife told him he was paying money to die. She taught school and had a way of making sense about things. Not that he was thinking about quitting.

She'd shake her head when he grabbed his pack and lighter and made for the backyard. But he figured Monroe was a better place than most to put money toward your own slow death.

Around here, it was practically a community tradition.

Simon took his $500, bought a piece of a package, camped out in his kitchen and chopped it up with baby laxative.

Fuck the ex-wife, fuck the landlord. Fuck the water bill. Something else was happening.

His cousin Kirby was the hook-up for the package, and now Kirby found some boys to flip it, taking bundles of ten or twenty bags and coming back a couple of hours later with cash. Simon turned that $500 into $2,000 in three days.

That was another thing the old man had said: "Money makes money, Si. Money makes money."

Real good advice.

Simon was out of the drug business just as quick as he was in it. No percentage in a game where the players shoot each other over next to nothing. That shit was for younger men.

Instead, Simon went down to Ray's, played pool, drank a little,

and waited. He didn't put the word out that he had money to
lend. That would have made him look overeager, and might
also draw the attention of violent, larcenous young men. He was
patient. Nice and slow.

Hey, Si: Don't fuck her all at once, you know?

On the third night, Simon was playing pool with an
acquaintance when the man, unprompted, spoke of money
troubles. Simon heard him out, shook his head in sympathy,
said nothing. They played some more, and the man spoke again.
This time Simon nodded thoughtfully and said, "You know,
maybe I could help you out."

The acquaintance was skeptical.

"It's true," said Simon. "Came into a little bit of money myself
not too long ago. I'm saying, you're hurting, I could maybe let
you hold some of it."

"Yeah?" said the man. "What you want for it?"

Simon furrowed his brow like he was confused. Now the
acquaintance was a little irritated.

"Shit," the man said. "Bet you take ten percent, just like the
gas station man. More, I bet."

He shook his head, lined up his next shot.

"I don't need that kind of bullshit."

"No," said Simon, "it ain't like that. I don't want nothing on
top of what I'm giving you. You just take it and get me back
down the line."

Simon paused. His pool partner had forgotten the shot. Now
he was standing up, looking straight at Simon.

Simon said: "I just got to make sure you pay me back, is all."

"Yeah?" said the acquaintance. "How you do that?"

Simon smiled.

"You got a car?"

The dead man had been attacked with something heavy; judging
by the width and depth of the holes in his face and head, the
amount of blood, it might have been a hammer. Some of the
neighbors had heard a scuffle and bursts of shouted profanity,
but by the time they'd turned their outside lights on there was
only a dead man on the ground, lots of blood, and the fading

sound of footsteps disappearing into the night.

Most of the neighbors knew the dead man. His name was Davis, lived a few blocks over. Probably walking home from Ray's, where he liked to play pool and often drank too much to drive. Good guy. Wife, kids. Out of steady work for a couple months now, but he still got up every day and tried.

Colclough thought: *All a man can do.*

He called dispatch from the radio in his car, asked them to tell the County Sheriff to send a forensics team over—not that there would be much to look for—and call the medical examiner, too.

He lit another cigarette and got ready to go see the family.

Simon learned about cutouts, if you can believe it, working as a janitor. This was some years ago.

The fabrication plant had just shut down, and at the time Simon was desperately in need of work. He saw the ad in the paper—bank in need of cleaning crew—and figured, hey, worse places to work than a bank, right?

Thing was: they worked *in* the bank, but they didn't work *for* the bank.

Simon learned this about a month in, when another guy on the crew broke his hand. The guy couldn't clean much with one hand, but he thought maybe the bank would hold his job until he healed up. So he went and talked to the branch manager.

The branch manager said: You see our name on your paycheck? No, right? Because you don't work for us. We contract this shit out. You work for someone else.

So the guy went to talk to the cleaning services contractor. And they said: Yeah, our name is on your paycheck. But we don't run this shit directly. You got to talk to the guy runs your cleaning crew.

So the guy went to talk to the crew boss—this was the man who'd hired them in the first place—and the crew boss said: Hey, the bank wants someone can clean tomorrow. Not someone can clean in a month or two, know what I mean? Hey, tough break, my man.

Simon heard the story from the guy with the broken hand, and he learned: Put some people between you and whatever shit you want done. That way it gets done without you getting all mixed up in *how* it gets done.

The guy Simon played pool with down at Ray's, he took $200. His name was Davis. And when it came time to do the work, Simon asked his cousin Kirby to look into it, but not directly. So Kirby passed the word to another guy he knew, and that guy passed it to some dope fiend who'd do anything for a hundred bucks.

When the dope fiend did Davis, Simon was down at Ray's, alibi'd up tighter than a virgin ass. Kirby was at his cousin's house, and the guy who paid the dope fiend was someone else all together—and what's a dope fiend going to remember about anything, anyway?

So Simon got it done, but he didn't get mixed up in the how. He stayed away from that.

Shame about Davis, sure. He was an okay guy.

But, shit, Simon didn't want the money. He wasn't looking for that $200 back.

Simon wanted the car.

About a week after they put Davis in the ground, Simon went to see the man's wife. He showed her the car title her husband had signed over.

"He didn't tell you, huh?" he said. "Yeah, he was having some money troubles. Said he wanted something new, anyway. I was letting him hold on to it for a week or so, just until he found something else."

"What'd you give him for it?" asked the wife.

"Thousand dollars," said Simon. Then he paused a second. "You must've seen some of that money, right? He buy some nice things all of a sudden?"

"I ain't seen a cent," she said, shaking her head. "Goddamn it, Davis."

Simon shook his head, too. He knew about husbands and wives. After all, he had been married once—and he wasn't married now. He told all this to Davis's widow, who took it in, accepting. She knew how men were.

She handed over the keys, and Simon put the car on the

lawn in front of his house. Went down to the county assessor and paid the taxes on the car, went to the DMV and got a new title. Bought one of those FOR SALE signs at the hardware store, scratched $1,500 on it. Figured he'd get a thousand after negotiating.

A week later he took $1,200 for the car. By then he had another $900 out on the street, split three ways. Shit, one of Davis's buddies had come knocking on his door. Simon thought the man was there to kill him.

"Heard you lending out money," the man said.

Simon smiled, invited the man in, gave him some ice water.

"Sure," he said. "Davis, he was a good man. Shame what happened. Least I can do, help out a friend of his."

Simon kept the smile on his face.

"You got a car?"

Ten days after the murder, Colclough stopped in to update Davis's widow on the case. Truth be told, there wasn't anything to pass along; he'd hit a wall almost from the start, which was why he was back with the widow, giving it one last try. There'd been another body on the south side two nights ago, and Davis was about to become priority zero.

The widow had nothing much to say. Didn't seem too happy with her recently departed husband. Grumbling, slamming the refrigerator shut.

"Now we ain't even got a car," she said.

Colclough asked for the story about that, and she told him. Figuring it was worth a shot, he went to see this guy Simon. Sure enough, the car the widow had described was out front of his house, FOR SALE sign on the windshield.

He knocked on the door. The guy smiled, invited him in. Average-looking guy, nothing special about him. Yeah, he said, he'd lent Davis some money, Davis had put his car up as collateral. Yeah, he had the title, no problem. Sure, he could account for his whereabouts on the night of the crime. Shame about Davis. Good guy.

Colclough checked up on Simon Bridge driving back to the station. No paper on the guy. Clean as anything.

Tough break for the widow, though, to lose the husband and then the car.

Who said life was easy?

Simon took it slow. Bit by bit, little at a time. The summer wound down, and he let the days and weeks pass.

Two of the guys who'd taken his money, he let them pay it back when they had it. He let Davis's buddy hold $200 for more than a month, never even bothered him about it. Waited until the man showed up at his door, took the wad of fives and tens and twenties. Shook the man's hand. No problem.

The third guy—the one who took $500—he let him hold it for a few weeks, and then he passed the word to Kirby. Kirby passed it down the line, and there it was.

No coincidence that this guy had the nicest car.

This time it was a different dope fiend, and this time he did it with a gun. Caught him right outside his house one morning. Car pulled up, handful of shots, sped away.

Awful shame, but nothing to do with whoever that crazy man was, killed someone with a hammer a month or so ago.

Hey, shit, sometimes people get shot.

South side of Monroe is a dangerous place to live.

Three months later, Simon's landlord was paid, his ex-wife was happy, the lights stayed on, the city wasn't charging him late fees on the water bills. He walked back into that loan office and paid off the principal and the interest. Kirby was taken care of—he had money in his pocket, and besides, he was cold as they come. He liked the idea of doing dirt.

Simon had four cars parked in front of his house now, each one in the $5,000 range.

"Si," his dad had told him, right before they locked him up, "in America, you can accomplish anything."

Real good advice.

Colclough spent most of his time on the south side. Summer turned into fall, winter knocked on the door, and people kept robbing each other, killing each other, quarreling over one another's wives and daughters.

He figured he wouldn't be out of work any time soon.

It must have been January when he passed Simon Bridge's house again, just randomly, driving back to the station to talk with the witnesses patrol had rounded up from a knife attack.

No one had died. So that was something.

What caught Colclough's eye driving past were the three cars on the man's front lawn. He slowed down and scoped the prices: $5,000; $6,500; $4,500.

Man took a liking to the car business, Colclough thought.

He'd thought about changing careers a time or two himself, tell you the truth.

Might help him cut down on the smoking. Make his wife happy.

Near the start of his shift one day in March, Colclough dropped in on his friend Victor, who managed one of the loan offices on Broad Street. It rankled Colclough more than a little to walk underneath that blinking sign out front—$$ Right Now— but Victor was a working guy, running the branch for a big company and trying to stay above water like everyone else, so Colclough figured he couldn't blame his friend for making a living.

He'd caught another murder last night, regular guy shot to death outside the gas station over on Pinckney. The counterman had heard the shots, hit the floor, and called the cops when he was sure everything was finished.

No witnesses. No cameras. No physical evidence. No nothing.

Colclough figured it could've been a random slight that sparked the killing, or else a simmering dispute from the neighborhood or a bar. Shit, could've been over nothing at all.

One human being emerges from the void, ends the life of another, and then disappears into the darkness.

South side of Monroe is a dangerous place to live.

Colclough thought stopping in to see Victor might give him some perspective, remind him that there were still plenty of people around here just trying to live life and make something for their families. Hell, most people were like that. It's just that the bad ones crossed a cop's radar more often than the others.

He and Victor shot the shit, locked up the store, hung around in the parking lot for a while.

"Shit," said Victor. "You wouldn't believe how many people out there just dying to sign their lives away. I had a guy in here the other week, wanted to put up his car, take his cash, and buy a new car. Right here from the lot."

Victor laughed. Colclough shook his head.

"No kidding," said Victor. "I asked him how much he was looking for, he asked me how much is that Jeep out there, the blue one with the leather. You believe that?"

"Yeah," said Colclough. "I believe it."

He paused.

"So you sell him the car?"

"What you think?" said Victor. "Course I sold him the car. You know this business, man. It'll be back on the lot in six months, along with the one he put up for the loan in the first place."

Colclough said nothing. Victor, sensing his discomfort, spoke quickly.

"You know how it is, Reg. Company don't want the money back from these people. They want cars out on the lot. And these people come in here, they can't wait to give 'em to us."

Victor started to walk toward his own car, then stopped, shook his head, turned back to Colclough.

"Only way we'd take these cars quicker is if we killed them right when they signed the papers. Know what I mean?"

Colclough nodded, preoccupied, and Victor got in his car and drove away. Something flashed for Colclough. A door opened, a drawer that should've been closed but wasn't, a piece that seemed to belong somewhere, but he couldn't quite place it.

Then it was gone.

Colclough lit a cigarette, leaned back against the hood of his car, and watched the street.

Charles Roland lives in an area convenient to several major southern cities. His work has appeared in *Workers Write! Tales from the Casino*, *Mystery Weekly Magazine*, Akashic Books'"Mondays are Murder" series, *Switchblade Magazine*, and more. He can be reached at charlesrolandauthor.com or charlesrolandauthor@gmail.com.

Classic Pulp

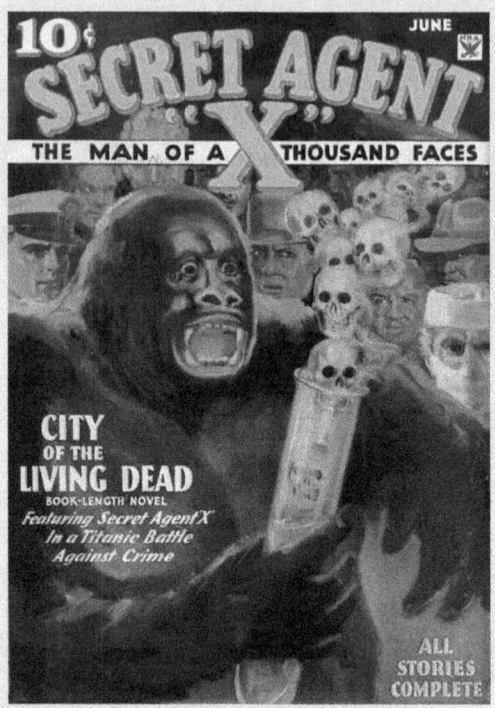

Following is a reprint of a story that originally saw print in the pulp magazine *Secret Agent X* June 1934. "No Living Witness" was an early work by Emile C. Tepperman (1899–1951) whose pulp fiction career ran from 1933 through the early 1940s. He wrote stories for several series including *Operator 5*, *The Spider*, and the Suicide Squad for *Ace G-Man*.

His Secret Agent X stories are considered by some as precursor to his work for *Operator 5*. His 13-part Purple Invasion series for *Op 5*, written under the house name Curtis Steele, is considered some of his best work.

His Ed Race stories feature a juggler who moonlights as a detective, appearing as a backup series in *The Spider* magazine from 1934 to 1939.

There is little information online about the writer, but he apparently moved from pulp magazines to radio scripts for programs like *Suspense* and *Gang Busters* later in his career.

Every crime has its victim.

No Living Witness
by Emile C. Tepperman

Cronin jabbed his automatic in the man's stomach. The street, close to the water front, was dimly lit, deserted at night. Cronin's thick upper lip curled back mercilessly from discolored teeth.

"Stand still, guy. Don't raise your hands—just keep 'em where they are. Only don't make no funny moves, see?" He accompanied the admonition with a jab of the gun.

The victim was short, lean, and hard- featured. He evidently knew all about what a Colt can do to your insides if it's fired with the muzzle against your stomach. For he stopped perfectly still.

"If this is a holdup, you can have my dough. There's a ten dollar bill in my pants pocket."

"That's all I need," said Cronin. "Turn around."

The other turned, very carefully.

Cronin dug his hand into the man's pocket and dragged out the ten dollar bill, keeping the gun handy. He pocketed the bill, and suddenly his big hamlike arm encircled the little man from behind. He almost lifted him off his feet, and whispered in his ear, "I'm gonna knock you off, fella. Jake Cronin never leaves a living witness!"

The lean man squirmed, his hands clawing at the implacable arm about his neck. He tried to talk, but only a hoarse cackle gurgled out of his larynx.

Cronin's eyes glittered with killer's lust. He gloated, his lips close to the other's ear. "In case it makes you feel better, you ain't bein' rubbed out by any ordinary stickup. I'm the guy that pulled the Associated Jewelers job. That was a fifty grand haul. I just gotta have some spending money till the fence comes through with the dough for the swag."

The little fellow's face was purpling. He raised his heels in the air and drummed frantically at Cronin's shins. The sudden pain of the kicking heels drew an oath from the killer's lips. His arm tightened viciously. There was a ghastly crunching snap, and the little man ceased struggling. Cronin expelled his breath in a wheeze and dropped the inert body. It sprawled slackly on the pavement, the head tilted back at a gruesome angle.

The man was dead, all right. Cronin knew a broken neck when he saw one. Stooping, he started to go through the dead man's pockets. There was an interesting bulge under the vest, but he was interrupted. Hard heels turned the far corner of the block, and he recognized the figure that passed under the street lamp. It was Detective Sergeant Pell.

Cronin cursed and melted into the doorway from which he had ambushed his victim. He felt his way through a black hallway, out into a back yard, over a fence and into an alley that led to the street beyond. As he emerged, he heard the blast of a police whistle. He grinned. That would be Pell, finding the body. Well, let him find it. They'd have to chalk up another murder to the unknown "Strangler's" account.

He strode swiftly away. A few blocks west he pulled the brim of his hat down over his eyes and entered a drug store. He bought a couple of packages of cigarettes, changed the ten dollar bill, and went into a phone booth. He dialed 211 and, when he got the long distance operator, he asked for a Chicago number. He got his connection, and a thin, rasping voice said, "Hello."

"This is—you know who," said Cronin,

"callin' from New York."

"Gott!" said the voice. "Not Cro—"

"Shut up, you fool! You want to advertise it? It's bad enough I had to call you up. I was sick and tired of hiding out in that stinking boarding house room for five days. And no dough. When I gave you them sparklers, you promised to send me the cash as soon as you got back to Chi. Well, where is it?"

The voice shrilled despairingly. "Gott! Don't yell like that! I told you it might take me a couple of days to raise the money. That's why you held out two of the stones. You were going to pawn them, no?"

"Yes, and all the hock shops were wised up. I couldn't take a chance. If the cops caught on I was in New York, they'd figure

me sure for that job. I'm supposed to be up in the mountains.
I had to go out and get me some spending money on the q. t.
tonight. So well, where's the dough?"

The operator broke in. "Your time is up, deposit ninety cents
for one minute more, sir."

Cronin thumbed three quarters, a dime and a nickel into the
slots, and heard the other saying, "I raised twenty grand for that
stuff this morning, and sent it with a guy named Gadwin. He's
flying to New York—started early this morning. He should be
there by now. Hurry up back and you'll maybe meet him."

"You sure you gave this guy Gadwin my right address,
Dutchy?"

"Yes, yes. The right address he's got written down, with that
phony name you're using."

"Okay," said Cronin. "I hope you ain't stringin' me, Dutchy. If
you are—"

He hung up and strode out, keeping his hat brim low.

With the change of his ten dollar bill, he stepped into a lunch
wagon and downed a plate of ham and eggs, two cups of coffee,
and a cut of apple pie. He bought a newspaper and a fifteen-cent
cigar, and strolled back to his rooming house.

Two-thirty-one Ellery Street, where he was temporarily
stopping under the name of Jonas, was one of a row of
bedraggled, crumbling four-story houses not far from the water
front. Each one sported an eight-step stoop and a "furnished
room" sign.

With his usual caution, he surveyed the street from the
doorway of the corner store, and seeing that it was clear, walked
swiftly to number two-thirty-one and ascended the stoop. He
stepped into the dark hallway and stopped, motionless, his
hand arrested in mid-air toward the shoulder clip where his
automatic rested.

The powerful beam of a flashlight caught him full in the eyes.
A moment later the hall light was switched on, the flashlight off,
and his blinking eyes discerned Detective Sergeant Pell, covering
him with a very steady thirty-eight.

"W-what's the big idea?" he mumbled.

Sergeant Pell was grim, the bleakness of his face denying the

levity of his words. "Well, look who's here! If it ain't Jake Cronin in the flesh! And here I was thinking you were far away in the mountains!" While he talked, he frisked him deftly, and took the automatic.

"How'd you know I was here?" Cronin asked, dry-mouthed.

"Just an accident, Jake, just an accident. I wasn't looking for you. But now I know you're in town, I'm beginning to get ideas about that Associated Jewelers holdup, Monday, where the girl cashier was killed. Looks just like it might be one of your jobs. Let's go up to your room and kind of glance it over."

Cronin felt a thick sensation in his chest as he led the way upstairs with Pell's gun an inch from his spine. The two diamonds he had held out were pasted to the bottom of the bureau drawer in his room. A good place to hide them from the landlady or a casual visitor, but they would never escape Pell's practiced search.

"How—how did you find this joint?" he demanded again, over his shoulder.

"It's funny about that," said Pell. "I wasn't looking for you at all. I was looking for a bird named Jonas. You see, I ran into a guy with a broken neck down by the water front. He had a wallet pinned under his vest. In the wallet was twenty thousand berries in big bills, and a card with a name written on it—Jonas, two-thirty-one Ellery Street. So I moseyed over, looking for Jonas, and who comes walking in behind me but Jake Cronin!"

Cronin stopped short on the staircase, his face gray with the realization of what he had done. He turned quickly, his arm coming backward in a short arc. His elbow jabbed Pell in the mouth, and the detective was thrown against the wall. Cronin faced him snarling. His right fist, balled into a vicious weapon of hard knuckles, was coming up in a smashing uppercut, when Pell's gun began to roar. Three times it kicked as he pulled the trigger. The slugs caught Cronin in the chest, and he toppled down the steps with a frightful cry that was drowned by the reverberations of the gunshots in the narrow hallway. He was dead when he hit the landing.

Woe unto them who would judge a stranger with little to no knowledge of what a stranger is capable of . . .

A Long Journey's End
by Matthew X. Gomez

Ariadna shielded her eyes as she stared up at the rough wooden palisade of Briarwood as merchants and travelers bustled past her. Most gave her some distance, the red cords wrapped around the hilts of her twin short swords marking her as a journeywoman duelist and not someone to be trifled with. She tried to remember what the town looked like when she left ten years ago and frowned, the creases around her eyes deepening. It looked bigger, dirtier, more crowded than she remembered. She adjusted the satchel hanging off her shoulder and gave the rein attached to her mule a hard tug.

"Business?" the guard asked, scratching the back of his neck. Ariadna noted the rust on his mail, the dirt caked under his nails, and the way he eyed her up and down in a way that made her want to reach for her blades.

"Coming home," she replied. Her hands drifted to her sword belt.

The guard snorted. "Careful wearing those in town, lass. Some men might take it amiss, a woman putting on airs."

Ariadna offered a knife of a smile that didn't touch her green eyes. "They can take it amiss as much as they want, but I earned these cords."

The guard raised an eyebrow. "Body guard work?"

Ariadna shrugged. "Some, sure. Also caravan work, champion, and judicial disputes."

The guard nodded, standing a little straighter. "How long are you planning to stay?"

Ariadna narrowed her eyes. "Indefinitely. Told you, I'm going home."

The guard shook his head. "Baron don't like idlers and loiterers. You stay here, you're going to have to find work. And it's two silver to enter."

Ariadna resisted the urge to draw her swords. She saw a nearby merchant press two clipped coppers into another guard's hand for entrance. Instead she produced two silvers from her belt pouch. "Maybe I'll apply to be a guard, if the pay is so good," she hissed before pressing deeper into the city.

Despite the time that had passed, Ariadna found herself walking familiar streets, her mule following after. She garnered a few curious looks from others, but no one impeded her progress. A fifteen-minute walk found her outside her childhood home. It looked smaller, more ramshackle than she remembered it, but then she had seen the gleaming marble walls of Garantia, the azure rooftops of Duskwall. Briarwood was a backwater in comparison. The training yard was covered with leaves, the posts nicked and chipped from years of abuse. She remembered peeking out through a crack in the door, watching her father run his students through their drills. She also remembered his cold anger at discovering her practicing on her own, his oath that no daughter of his would ever carry a sword.

A small streamer of smoke drifted up against the painted sunset sky. She tied the mule to a post, pulled the saddlebag off, and hefted it on to her shoulder. She raised her hand to push the door open, decided to knock instead.

"I ain't got your money, Samuel!" a cracked and raw voice called from inside. "Told you that yesterday."

Ariadna pushed the door open. Her father sat in his chair by the window, a knife on the table next to him. He looked old, partially collapsed on himself. His hands were gnarled, the fingers partially curled. It was evident he hadn't shaved in a few weeks, and from the smell he hadn't bathed in at least that long. He stared at her with rheumy eyes, blinking against the light pouring into the house. She stepped further into the room, the dust kicked up, threatening to choke her.

Her father looked, blinked, and rubbed his eyes. "I don't

recognize you. Samuel hiring girls now?" His hand scrabbled for the knife, knocked it on the floor. Ariadna approached, picked the blade up from the floor. The last time she saw her dad, they spat curses at each other like a couple of alley cats. Two dishes had broken when he hurled them at her. A final biting remark and he refused to watch as his only blood in the world left him behind. She knew because she had turned back at the last moment, cursing herself for her weakness. The sight of his back spurred her on out of the city, her eyes filling with tears she refused to shed. She'd already stashed the blades in her baggage on the mule.

"It's me, Da. Ariadna."

Her father paused reaching for the knife, sat back in his chair, and made a noise like he'd just been gut punched. "Ariadna? Didn't think you'd ever come back here. Been what, ten years?"

Aridan nodded, fighting back a sob.

"Speak up, girl. My ears aren't what they used to be. Hells, nothing about me is like it used to be."

"Yes, Da," she replied, finding her voice.

He leaned forward, eyes squinting. "You're still carrying the blades."

Ariadna nodded. "Yes." Her mouth quirked up into a smile. "Got my journey cords, too."

Her father pushed himself to his feet and took a step forward. Aridana wasn't sure what she expected, but to be folded into his arms was near the bottom of the list. The last time he'd hugged her had been, when exactly? Before her mother passed, surely. She remembered fitting her head under his chin and now her eyes easily cleared the top of his head.

"Why did you come back?" he asked, finally releasing her and slumping back in the chair.

Ariadna moved over to the fire, poked the embers to life. "Like you said, it's been ten years. I figured it was time to come home."

She heard a dry rattle and only when she turned to look, seeing her father shaking in his chair, did she realize he was laughing. "Hoping I was dead?"

"No," she said. "Though I was worried you might be. Who's

this Samuel then?"

Her father waved a hand and folded back in on himself. "Local tough guy. Thinks he's a swordsman. Built himself up a little gang, mostly of people too scared to stand up to him or too stupid to see he's nothing but a couple of flash moves and empty bravado. Tough enough to give one old man trouble though."

"And the local guards?"

Her father made a sound in the back of his throat and spit out a wad of phlegm onto the floor. "Rat bastards, the lot of them. Baron's only interested in making sure he's got his coin and Samuel isn't enough of an idiot to not make sure he's not paid up."

Ariadna wrinkled her nose. "But didn't you used to train his guards? Spar with him? You'd think there'd be . . ."

Her father shook his head. "You're thinking of the old man. He died, what, six years ago? No, this is his brat. Spent the first two years purging anyone not seen as sufficiently loyal. Let the local gangs gather power so long as they didn't threaten his base. And now? He can't move against any of them on the chance that the others would move against him."

Ariadna looked around the room. There wasn't much there. The same rough wooden furniture she remembered from her childhood. The same crude pottery. Some herbs and root vegetables hanging from the ceiling. "So what's Samuel's trouble with you?"

Her father snorted. "He thinks I've got some coin buried. Thinks because he's the big man in this part of Briarwood, he's entitled to it. Truth to tell, girl, you picked a bad time to come back."

Ariadna smiled. Her father recognized it as the same sort of smile she put on as a child when she was about to get up to some sort of mischief. The kind of smile she wore as a child when she practiced in the yard when she thought he wasn't watching. He knew she wouldn't be dissuaded and the only real choice was to help her or not.

"Where can I find Samuel?" she asked, fingers tapping on the hilts of her swords.

Ariadna stepped into The Rogue's Club, the smell of spilled whiskey and unwashed bodies assaulting her before she even stepped over the threshold, her eyes watering from the stench. Samuel wasn't hard to spot, holding court in the center of the common room with a serving girl perched on his knee and a stein in one massive hand. Even sitting down, he dominated the four men with him, his massive frame overflowing the chair, some fat to be sure, but muscle under that. His face was mostly hidden by a coarse black beard shot through with grey. He looked up when Ariadna walked over to the bar, nudging the weasel-looking man next to him with his elbow.

"Ale," Ariadna said, placing a silver coin on the bar.

"Don't reckon I know you," the weasel man said, sidling next to her. Four daggers were sheathed in a bandoleer across his chest. "This here is our territory, and we make sure to know everyone."

"That a fact?" Ariadna accepted the ale from the barkeep and took a sip. She screwed her face up at the bitter taste and wondered where they were getting their supply and what was being put in it. She decided she was better off not knowing.

Weasel-face tapped his fingers on the top of the bar, his finger nails cracked and black. "Are you passing through or looking to stay?"

"Thought I'd stay. Reestablish my roots."

"Reestablish . . . ? You're from Briarwood."

She nodded, fingers closing around the handle of the stein. "Born and raised here. Been gone for a time. Funny, it's still as much of a shithole as it ever was."

"So, looking for work?" Weasel-face asked, glancing down at her swords. "There's a bit of work for a woman who knows her way around a blade," he added with a leer.

Ariadna shook her head, turning to look down at Weasel-face. "Thought I'd go into business for myself. Take over from my da."

"Your da?"

"Mateu Cardona."

"Oh, shi—"

Weasel-face didn't get to finish his statement as Ariadna

slammed her stein into his face. He fell down with a howl, clutching his broken jaw and spitting teeth.

She stepped over him for the exit as Samuel and the rest of his crew erupted from their seats, spilling the unfortunate serving girl onto the floor. Stepping out into the night air, she drew a deep breath and rested her hands on the hilts of her swords, her thumbs running over the red cords.

Samuel stepped into the street first, his face twisted in anger. "I don't know who you think you are . . ."

"Ariadna Cardona, daughter of Mateu Cardona. Adept of the sword." She tapped her fingers against the hilts. "And you are a scum sucking piece of trash." She smiled, her eyes gleaming from the lamps lit around the courtyard. "I think that takes care of introductions don't you?"

The first gang member rushed at Ariadna, a short spear in one hand and a small shield in the other, held close to his body. Ariadna's blades spun in her hands, one knocking the spear to the side and the other driving over the shield and into the spearman's shoulder. She pushed off, going low and spiking her blade into the side of his knee. She spun off, slipping under an axe strike from one of the other gang members. She sucked in her stomach from a disemboweling attack, then thrust her left hand blade into the gang member's chest, punching through his leather jerkin. Blood bubbled up from his mouth, and she pulled her blade free and spun around his body, putting the soon-to-be-dead man between her and his friends. The one she stabbed in the shoulder and knee was down on the ground howling in pain and wouldn't be getting back up again.

Weasel-face came at her from around his friend, two daggers flying from his hands. Ariadna flicked her wrists, the daggers spinning away from her. Then he was on top of her, twin blades in his hand, flicking, testing, and slicing. She parried, twisted, and backed up, her arms stinging each time Weasel-face's blades kissed her skin, opening up red lines on tanned skin. She launched a kick at his knee, and he twisted his leg to get it out of the way. That left him open for her well-timed thrust, her blade moving like a needle in and out of his arm, severing tendons and breaking bones. Weasel-face howled and dropped his dagger. He stumbled and fell back onto his rear. He scrabbled backward, still clutching his wrist.

Ariadna stepped toward him, blood streaming down her arms, but stopped short. Samuel stood there, waiting. A two-handed war sword rested on his shoulders as he stood watching, scowling.

"Those cords aren't for show, are they?" he asked. He rolled his shoulders, brought the war sword into a guard position.

"You're okay with your people fighting and dying for you?" she asked. She wavered, feeling light-headed from blood loss.

Samuel watched as the axe-wielder fell to his knees and then on to his face, as Weasel-face scrambled to his feet and sprinted into the dark. "Always more where they came from," he replied with a shrug. "I didn't know Mateu had a daughter."

"I've been . . . away."

"So I see. Your old man teach you how to use a blade?" He started circling her, drawing closer, the tip of his sword pointed unwavering at her throat.

"Not as such." She turned in profile, projecting as small a target as possible. "I used to watch him teach. Rest I picked up on the way."

Samuel chuckled. "I have to admit, I'm impressed. You don't see too many journeymen able to take on four and survive."

"Your men were undisciplined. If they'd worked together, I'd be dead right now. Same is true if you'd helped them."

"Could be." Samuel grinned through his beer, a flash of brilliant white in his dark beard. "But that wouldn't have been as much fun."

He lunged, arms extending out, using his height and reach to close the distance. Ariadna caught the blow on both her blades, the shock running up the blades to her arms and making her teeth ache. She pushed Samuel's sword to the side, ran up to him, her blades grinding against her. He kicked out at her, but she snapped her left blade out, catching him in the thigh as the air whooshed out of her when his heel hit her stomach. She was knocked back, but the blow was weaker than it might have been. Samuel stared at her, her blade still sticking out of the side of his upper thigh.

Samuel took a step toward her, but his leg buckled, unable to support his weight. Dropping to a knee, his lips pulled back in a snarl.

"Come on then," he shouted at her.

Ariadna spun her remaining blade in her hand, and took a step, pausing as the world swam and spun around her. She'd need to find a barber when all was said and done.

Samuel leveraged himself to his feet, using his blade to prop himself up. "Come on!" Spittle sprayed from his mouth.

Ariadna approached, her feet dragging in the dirt. Samuel tried to hack at her, but his leg didn't want to cooperate and he fell forward.

"Wait, wait, wait," he spluttered, words half-choked in the dirt.

She frowned at him, then drove her sword down, planting it by his head. She reached down and yanked out her other blade with a twist before walking away, swaying and stumbling into the twisted streets of Briarwood.

Ariadna woke up, her eyes making out the wooden cross beams of her father's home. Her home. Her bed.

"You're awake," her father grunted. He poked at the fireplace, slopped a bit of liquid from a kettle into a bowel. "Wasn't sure if you were going to make it. Looks like you ran into a case of knives."

"Not that far from the truth," she muttered, forcing herself to sit up. Her arms still stung, and looking down, she saw they were wrapped in white bandages tinged pink.

Mateu snorted. "Thought you had more sense than that. Then again, I didn't think you'd go and pick up the sword either."

"I'm your daughter."

Mateu grunted. "The more's the pity for you."

"Some gratitude." She took the bowl and lifted it to her lips, sipping the bone beef broth.

Mateu sank back into the chair by the fire. "I didn't ask for help."

"So what were you going to do, throw yourself on Samuel's sword?"

"I would have thought of something."

"Mmmhmm." She took another long sip of broth.

"So you'll be leaving again?" he asked after a long pause.

"Why would you think that?"

"Because . . . well, what are you are you going to do?"

"I have a bit of coin. Could always reopen the school."

Mateu laughed, harsh and bitter. "Who would learn from a journeywoman?"

"Look in my satchel bag."

Mateu limped over to her bag, rifled around in her bag before pulling out twin cords. He walked them closer to the fire, held them up the light.

"Purple cords?" he asked, disbelief evident on his worn features. "Why don't you have these on your blades?"

Ariadna set the bowl on the table next to the bed and leaned back into her pillow, closing her eyes. "Funny isn't it? No one really wants to bother a journeywoman. But a master? Everyone wants to prove a girl couldn't possibly have earned those, and if she did, well, everyone wants to say they took down a master. So I never took the old cords off." She tapped the side of her head. "The cords don't matter though, not really. They note skill with the blade, they don't give it. And sometimes, most times, it's better to be underestimated."

Mateu chuckled. "Sounds familiar. Can't imagine who taught you that."

"Oh, someone I knew, once upon a time." Her voice came soft and sleepy. "Wake me in the morning, and we'll see about getting some students. I imagine there are enough desperate souls willing to learn, even if it is from a woman."

Mateu nodded and stared into the fire, the wood crackling as the flame consumed it.

Matthew X. Gomez is a spec fic writer with an active blog and dozens of pieces available in both print and at his personal website (mxgomez.wordpress.com). He is a lifelong lover of fantasy and horror, especially that of the pulp genre. His work has appeared on the Dark Futures website (including the 12 piece serial *Burned Lands*), *Phase 2 Magazine*, in the *Midnight Abyss* anthology, and in the *Altered States II* anthology. He is the coeditor of the New Pulp magazine *Broadswords and Blasters*..

There is no such thing as security.

Tick-Tock in the House America Built

by Marc E. Fitch

Glen returned from the war a broken man and marred with occasional flashbacks, which thrust him back into the desert heat with its mix of blood and human stink and left him standing dazed and confused, unable to speak or move for long periods of time. For this reason, he was given medication and put on

disability for PTSD and received a check every month which
allowed him to stay in the house his grandfather had built in
the hills outside Bantam. He attended therapy for a number of
months and was educated in certain "grounding techniques"
which would help him control his occasional fugue states and
come back to reality. It was difficult because these fugue states
were often for extended periods of time and
when a person would try to wake him from
it, he would often lash out violently;
horrific images passed through his
mind as if he were being
tortured by some
sentient being

meant on doing him irrevocable harm.

For this reason, Glen received an animal trained to nuzzle its ward back into consciousness without worry that the patient would violently lash out. Oddly enough, those experiencing the pain of PTSD and these fits of psychosis would only lash out at other people and were remarkably surprised and put at ease when they came to and saw a dog or, in Glen's case, a pig.

It was quite the laugh among his fellow vets at the VA, and Glen smiled along with them in his usual All-American football player style, but he secretly resented the animal. The pig was named Tick-Tock. Glen wished he had a dog. The VA was fresh out of dogs. Pigs, being the smarter animal, were employed more often and to better effect with less cost of procurement and training. Thus, Glen had Tick-Tock the pig rather than Tick-Tock the dog. Eventually, the fellows at the VA had come to see the animal as a good omen. Tick-Tock, however, seemed indifferent to all of them, snuffling along the ground for whatever food morsels he could find and making small, grunting noises. Either way, as a companion, it was at least something to talk to when he was wandering alone in the halls of his grandfather's house. Tick-Tog dogged him everywhere. The pig kept him sane, more or less, with its ugly snuffling and waddling, despite its indifference to his fate.

Glen's grandfather had been a soldier in World War II and, after surviving the beaches of Normandy and losing his left leg to a mortar outside Berlin, returned to the States, built his own home, started a construction business, married, and had children. He lived into his seventies and occasionally talked of the war, but, more often than not, talked of church and his family. He was able to do all that having survived one of the bloodiest battles in history and a wooden leg. Glen was walking through hallways he didn't have the ability to construct with no family, no faith, and only a pig nipping at his heals. In this sense, the whole house was a crucible of guilt, embarrassment, and shame that he could not move on to create the American dream as his grandfather had done. The therapists told him that this was a new age, a different time. They said it was a different kind of war, that the notion of Good vs. Evil was no longer relevant and so soldiers could not create mythologies by which to understand and deal with their inevitable feelings of guilt and remorse. Glen told himself that it was all just shit. The world was shit and he was stuck in it. The pig snuffled at his feet and took his hand in its wet mouth, which Glen pulled away, somewhat irritated.

The house was old at this point and the foundation had cracked and the wood was beginning to weather. Glen would occasionally find a leak from the roof or faulty electrical outlet or a piece of molding pulled away from a doorway. He would consider repairing it, but always put it off until the next day and so on. With no job and nowhere to be at any particular time, it seemed to Glen that such matters were not matters of time but, rather, matters of desire and, at this point, he had little desire.

The second floor of his grandfather's house contained two extra bedrooms and a study that still retained his grandfather's war memorabilia. Glen rarely ventured to the second floor because of that room. However, following his weekly group therapy session, Glen returned home to find a small puddle in the living room, pooled on the hardwood floor, which Tick-Tock began lapping at. It had been raining fairly hard that afternoon. Glen ascended the steps to the loft above the living room to have a look at the ceiling. The paint had bubbled and the sheetrock was soaked through. He was going to have a hell of a mess to clean up. He uselessly pawed at the sloped ceiling and muttered some curses under his breath. He nudged Tick-Tock out of the way to give himself a little space. There was not much disability money to go around and the repairs would definitely hurt his budget. He hoped for some kind of insurance claim but knew in the back of his head that he was screwed.

"Gonna' go a little hungry this month," he said to the pig. One of the most convenient things about having a pig was that it would eat anything and everything and so Glen wasn't stuck buying special food developed by scientists for the discerning dog-lover. Tick Tock ate what came and was generally quite happy about it.

Glen passed by the half-open door of his grandfather's study and saw the flag inside, folded into a triangle revealing the stars and stripes in just the right proportion to give it the solemn appearance of patriotic duty and eternal reverence. It struck him for a moment, the sight of those colors folded into a triangle, and he immediately saw those same triangles being given to grieving widows and families of men he knew and fought with in Iraq. He saw mortars and IED's; he saw children strapped with bomb belts; he saw dust-storms and tracer rounds and heard screams of pain and pleas for mercy in languages that reached back thousands of years; he felt pain, smelled diesel, tasted blood, and saw missiles streaking down from unmanned drones to the laser pinpoint he placed on a sandstone home somewhere in Fallujah. He felt himself falling down a deep, irrevocable abyss.

It was then that his feet had reached the top of the staircase and Tick-Tock took Glen's hand in his wet mouth, pressing the flesh of his hand between its all-too-human teeth. Glen snapped out of his fugue, jerked his hand to his chest. His feet, wet from the leaking rain water, slid on the hardwood and Glen spun and fell backwards down the stairs, landing on his back, rolling over on his head, and snapping the vertebrae of this neck till finally coming to rest at the base of the staircase, feet on the floor, body sprawled out on the stairs face up. The last thing he heard before he blacked out was horrid squealing, like the sound of children burning.

It was dark when he woke and he could feel nothing. The world came back to him in shades of darkness. It was like blindness leaving him. He lay prone at the base of the old oak staircase and he moved his throbbing, aching neck so he could see the spindles tracing ornate vertical lines to the handrail, but he could move nothing else. He willed his arms to reach up, but they would not respond. He tried to move his legs, to wiggle his foot at the very least, but it was like he had forgotten how. No matter what neural pathways he implored his brain to find, there was nothing on the other end receiving that transmission. He lay for a moment. His mind raced. For some reason, he kept wondering what time it was. Time had stopped, or maybe he had stepped out of it, the way he stepped out of his corporeal body. It was a dreamscape—a nightmare—where time was of no consequence and movement was a thing left in another dimension. Fear ran through his mind—*I am alone.*

He heard a sound, a familiar snuffling and hooves on hardwood that sounded like a grandfather clock ticking away the hours in rapid succession. He saw Tick-Tock, floppy ears and beady eyes, with the semblance of actual, human emotion on his face.

Glen whispered his name and the pig took Glen's hand in his mouth, but Glen could not feel it and could not recoil away. The pig simply held his hand there for what seemed an eternity. Glen cried and then began to yell hopelessly for help. His voice echoed back to him. Tick-Tock squealed a horrendous sound.

"Help me somebody!" It was all he could do to force the air from his lungs and coarsen his dry throat. Grandfather built the house at the end of a long driveway. Grandfather liked the trees. Not even the sound of passing cars on the road made it through.

Glen weighed his options, which were practically none, and then ran the numbers in his mind as to what possible help could be summoned: middle of the night, in a house set back in the trees far from a lonely road. He might as well save his breath. His cell phone was on the kitchen counter through the doorway. Maybe if someone tried to reach him. . . . but then, when was the last time he received a call? Even the guys from the VA whom he occasionally spoke with did everything in text message. Gone were the days when an unanswered phone would cause curiosity or alarm. An unanswered text was forgotten as soon as the digital words left the screen, useless and impersonal. He weighed the chances of Tick-Tock pulling some black-and-white Lassie feat of heroism and erased that off the chalkboard of his thoughts. He almost had a bout of insane laughter at the idea of Tick-Tock trying to tell some passerby that Timmy had fallen in a well or fallen down the stairs. Dumb fucking hope. He and the pig were locked together in this house. He might as well have been Saddam at the bottom of that hole.

The shock wave passed and the inferno of fiery emotion followed; fear, anger, despair, a rethinking over and over of every decision he made that day, that week, that month, that lifetime and, had he the ability to move his arm, he would have gladly shot himself if the head. He cried. A deep heaving, choking cry, something he'd never done since the war, but probably should have. When the tears were gone, his mind ran to the fact that a single teardrop hung from the tip of his nose and he couldn't wipe it away. He cursed God. He cursed his family and his grandfather. He cursed his country and raged against the cosmos that had left him prone and helpless on a staircase. Tick-Tock took his hand in his mouth. "And fuck you, too," he said before he fell asleep from sheer emotional exhaustion.

Daylight. Time still unknown, but it was bright outside and the sunlight streamed through dirty windows. The dust danced in the air, then settled on his chest. His eyes adjusted to the light. A smell hit him. He strained his neck and looked down at his body. He had pissed and shit himself. Humiliation on top of it. If he was ever rescued, it would probably be by Miss America turned EMT and here he was, laying in his own filth comforted by a pig. He heard Tick-Tock in the kitchen, his hooves scraping along the linoleum. The sound of a turned over garbage can and his snuffling nose prodding through the empty bag. Glen's mouth was desert-dry, his tongue felt like sand grinding against the roof of his mouth. His lips stuck together and he had to tenderly pry them open with his tongue. Glen was starving and parched. Two days without food or water. His stomach churned and turned in on itself.

He also had a second dawning horror: he was taught some basic medical facts in the Army for aiding soldiers with combat wounds, including paralysis. A broken, paralyzed person can't move of their own accord. Left lying in a prone position too long caused the side of the body facing the ground to swell and begin to poison itself. He raised his neck as far as he could with painful needles dancing through his vertebrae, so that he could finally see his feet at the bottom of the stairs. They were like two pink balloons. At first, he didn't even recognize them. They were something foreign, no longer a part of his body, no longer a part of his being and maybe they never were. But now it looked like the skin was ready to break its stitching and pour out some ungodly mess of bodily fluids. He dropped his head back to the stairs in exhaustion. He heard the pig wandering somewhere in the empty house. His phone rang in the kitchen. It went to voicemail. Another voice talking into the empty ether. The sun was setting again. Darkness came.

He dreamed. His mind rummaging through memories and magically presenting them in some strange, dramatic fashion so that reality was the true illusion. The skies were green, painted in night vision, streaks of tracer rounds, like shooting stars. He floated miles overhead with crimson crosshairs painted on a target. Boom. Gone. No sound. All silence. He was walking through the sand completely naked except for his M-16 cradled in his arms like a newborn. In his nakedness, he approached Ramadhi. Eyes watched him, staring from beneath burqas and sweat stained brows. Up ahead lay the carrion dead of his platoon. A small Iraqi boy handed him a toy soldier, a gift from the soldiers to promote good will. He looked at the toy soldier, dressed in desert camo, lopsided helmet, smiling. He held it close and it burned like the desert sun. Something was in the desert. Out to the East beyond the horizon where he could not see; something was there whispering to him in a guttural language eons old but faintly recognizable. It was beckoning to him.

He woke to a snuffling sound, a ripping and tearing, and the dawn light opened his eyes to the confines of his own private hell. The dream left its indelible print of agony and confusion on his mind, fading like an echo. He heard the sound and thought, at first, someone had found him, kicked down the door, and plunged inside to find him prone on the staircase. But then he recognized the noise; Tick-Tock close by, munching on something. The pig's jaws were moving fast. Glen called out for the pig but there was nothing but the sound of chewing. Then he was suddenly jerked downward, his body sliding two steps closer to the floor, the back of his head bouncing off the wooden stairs. He saw the brown and pink flopping ears of Tick-Tock and his tiny black eyes. Glen raised his head as far as he could and looked down to his feet where the pig was quivering. Instead of his pink balloon feet, there were nothing but bloody stumps, pieces of his former self, hanging idly from bone that had been partially chewed through.

He screamed in the emptiness of the house his grandfather built. He screamed as if there was pain. He screamed because there was no pain. He screamed from the phantoms that were burrowing through the stump and up to his shivering brain. He screamed because there was no one to hear him.

Tick-Tock stopped momentarily and looked at him. There was red stain over his porcine mouth and the faint look of a piggly grimace. Glen stared into those beaded eyes. Was there a hint of comprehension? A hint of knowing? This was betrayal.

"You motherfucker! You ungrateful motherfucker!" He bellowed at the pig. "This? This is what you do to me? This is what I get?" Glen sucked down tears of rage. He spit and cursed God and country. He stared down at the snorting animal that now turned its attention back to his leg. He could see a dull red pool spread out from his leg like melting butter. His mind was light and shimmering like he had too many glasses of some champagne he could never afford. Bright lights danced in the darkness. A dinner party, perhaps. Beautiful women serving cocktails and appetizers he couldn't pronounce. He snapped out of his hallucinations and turned back toward Tick-Tock.

"Tick-Tock! No! Bad! No! Bad Tick-Tock!" He almost laughed and then almost cried and then almost raged again, but it all seemed far off now. The animal kept on eating, pulling his pant leg away in stitches, moving up his calf and on to his thigh, strong and meaty from miles of running in basic. He willed his body to move but it would not move. He willed himself to feel but he could not feel. He stared up at the rafters that his grandfather laid, at the plaster his grandfather smoothed with his own hand, at the dripping ceiling whose mildewed water was mingling with his blood on the floor. He watched Tick-Tock eat. Pigs will eat anything and everything they had said—ultimate consumers. Gangsters ditch bodies in pig pens in Italian villages so that the evidence is gone—bones and all.

He stared in rapt fascination. "Leave me my bones, Tick-

Tock," he said. But the pig did not look up and kept burrowing through his body like a rat through carrion. He put his head back and listened to the sound of it, that guttural grunting, that ancient language that he heard in his dreams; the sounds of masticating, eating, swallowing and snorting for breath when burying your face into the mess of it. That was the sound—the language—the desert horizon beckoning to him now. Here he was, stripped so naked that even his bones were exposed to the world, listening to this pig—his supposed protector—speaking to him of his own impending death.

He opened his eyes again. A figure from his nightmares stood in the room, gently swaying back and forth. Draped in black with only a fabric screen where the eyes should be, it was a strange inversion of the way a child might pretend to be a ghost with nothing more than a white bed sheet. It stood in the foyer and swayed in an unseen desert breeze. It wasn't Tick-Tock making the sounds now, it was this phantom and, somehow, he could see it working its mouth beneath the black linen, chewing, speaking.

Beckoning him. Drawing him.

He was walking naked through Ramahdi, stripped of skin. Cradling machined death. Spewing his worthless life from his mouth like bile.

And they were welcoming him into the horizon, into that place where the tall figure in nothing but black stood against the rising sun and blistering heat.

"No, Tick-Tock," he said, but he said it without conviction and his language was engulfed by the other. His eyesight was becoming a pinprick from down a deep well. The pig had moved up onto the stair, eating at his groin and hips.

The shrouded figure bent over him and he could see all of the world in its strange gaze; lost in a pit of despair, battling forces older than history itself. The phantom whispered things to him and they sounded like a pig chewing through meat.

The pig moved up another stair as it ate away at him. Its back pushed up against his fingers. Suddenly, to Glen's horror, his fingers registered a sensation.

Floating in the darkness, he felt the faint, stiff hairs that bristled from the back of the pig's neck. He felt the warm skin pushing up against his hand. It felt almost human.

Marc E. Fitch Marc E. Fitch is the author of the novels *Old Boone Blood*, *Paradise Burns* and *Dirty Water*, as well as the books *Paranormal Nation: Why America Needs Ghosts, UFOs and Bigfoot* and *Shmexperts: How Power Politics and Ideology as Disguised as Science*. Marc's fiction has appeared recently in *Pulp Modern*, *The Horror Library* vol. 6 and *Strange Beasties* among others. Marc lives and works in Connecticut.

© Marc E. Fitch

"My name is xzklz, from the Planet txkj.
I didn't come to kill Earthings. You all seem to be
doing a good job of that yourselves."

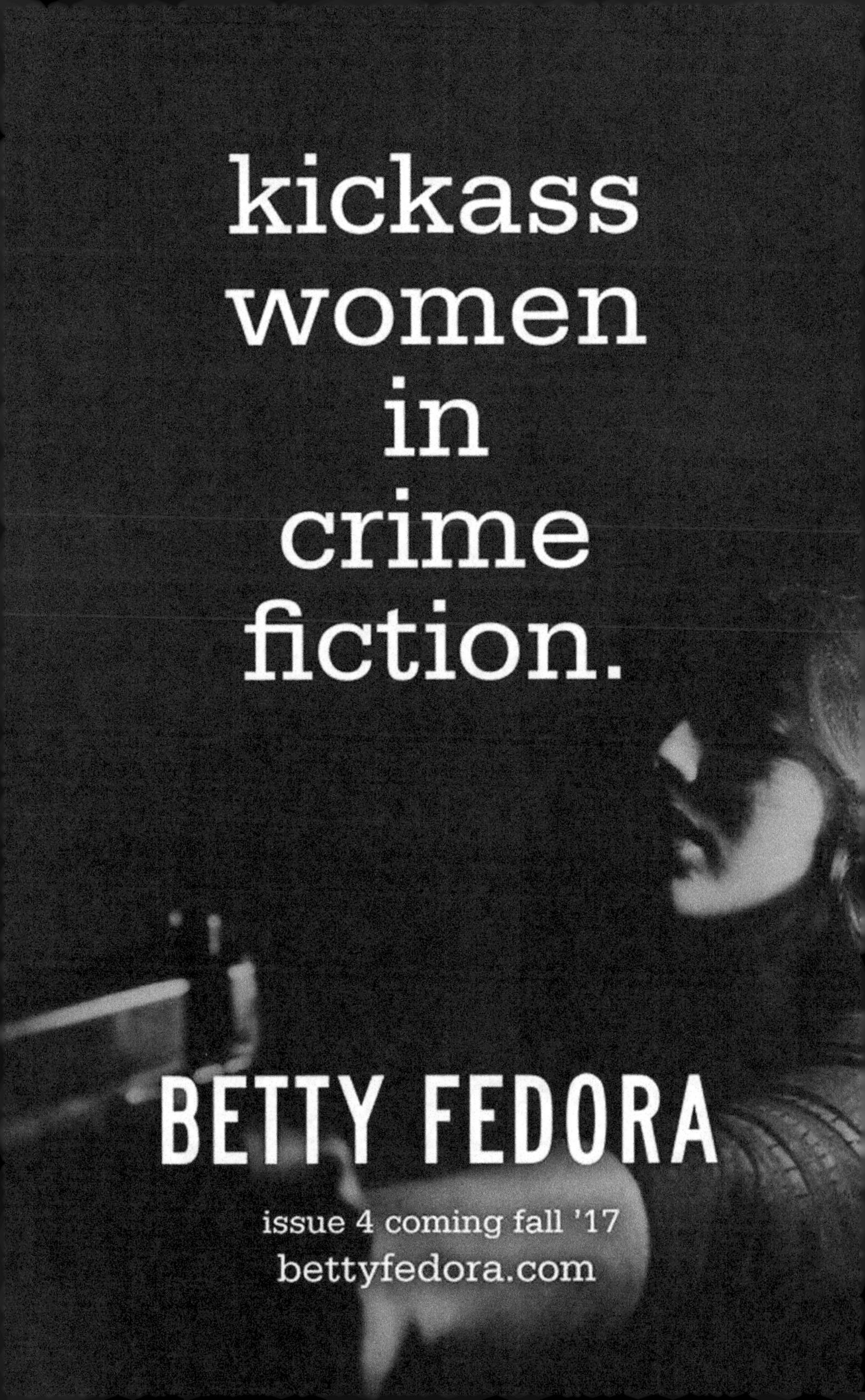
kickass
women
in
crime
fiction.
BETTY FEDORA
issue 4 coming fall '17
bettyfedora.com

Laziness will be the death of us all.

Double Jeopardy
by Susan E. Abramski

HAVE YOU EVER WISHED YOU COULD BE IN TWO PLACES AT ONCE?

Shit, yeah! Calvin silently replied to the advertisement in the classified section of *The Times-Courier*. I could've spent all my time at home listening to my wife babble at me about what a loser I am instead of going to work like a fool to keep a roof over her head and mine. Screwed her as often as she wanted, too, like that UPS guy she ran away with last week must have done. And I thought he kept showing up at the front door every day because she was just addicted to those home shopping channels!

EVER WISH YOU COULD BE TWO PEOPLE? the ad continued.

Even better. Could've screwed her and worked. Better still, screwed her sister and worked.

YOUR DREAM CAN NOW BECOME A REALITY!

Sure it can, dude. With enough whiskey, maybe. How much are they paying you to write this bullshit?

HOMOGENESIS CORPORATION HAS DEVELOPED A GUARANTEED, FOOLPROOF, PAINLESS WAY FOR THAT DREAM TO BECOME REALITY, RIGHT NOW!

Now Calvin was interested. This ad wasn't put out by some New Ager working out of their kitchen—this was a *Corporation*. Legitimate. With at least enough profit to be able to afford to run an ad in a major newspaper.

Never mind that he was now unemployed and that the last cent he had in the bank would probably end up going toward paying for a Caribbean roof over the heads of his wife and the UPS guy. Calvin was interested. For an opportunity like this, he could sell a few things.

FOR NO MONEY DOWN, WE WILL, WITHIN THE SPAN OF A MONTH, SUPPLY A GUARANTEED IDENTICAL, DNA-EXACT, INDISTINGUISHABLE DUPLICATE OF YOURSELF!!

This couldn't be a scam—papers vet their ads before they run them, don't they? Especially major newspapers. Their reputation depends on it, doesn't it? Therefore, Calvin was interested. He was definitely interested.

Irrevocably interested.

"Think of this, Calvin: From the moment your— 'clone,' shall we say—to make use of an archaic term—appears in public, you are as good as a retired man. You will become independently wealthy. Your time will be entirely your own, to do with as you please. Just consider it, Calvin. The world will be your Garden of Eden—Are you a religious man?—the way it was meant to be before all that 'condemnation' and 'tilling the land by the sweat of your brow' business. Let your clone do all the work while you sit back and rake in the rewards! Everyone will think it's you. *You'll* get all the credit. *And* all the glory."

"And all the money." Calvin made sure to emphasize this aspect.

"Of *course* all the money, Mister Michaels! That goes without saying! Why else would anyone do business with us?"

Calvin could think of several reasons, almost all of them illegal. He didn't mention any of them because *he* didn't want to be accused of having any illegal motives. "Beats the hell out of me, Mister." He replied instead, all innocence. "I'm sorry, I forgot what you told me your name was."

"I didn't, Mister Michaels. My oversight. You may address me as Mister Wright, to avoid any awkwardness. It would grieve me to make you in any way uneasy."

They weren't sure enough of getting his business to still be trying to kiss up to him, Calvin thought. Calvin liked being in the driver's seat. "Well . . . what about the little matter of cost? I don't even know if I can *afford* your service. Sounds like a very expensive proposition and I find myself a bit, er, 'financially embarrassed' at present. And if he . . . excuse me—*it*—is going to be my exact duplicate, won't it cost me to feed it? I've become rather fond of eating regularly, myself—that's what drove me to the classifieds section in the first place. Haven't had to look at the employment ads in years, but now I have to find something that pays enough to replace what that vortex of a female I married sucked out of my retirement fund, don't I?"

"You don't need to be employed to sign on with us, Mister Michaels. We're not looking for your money. *We* will pay *you*."

This was definitely in the "too good to be true" category that Calvin had made it his life's mission to avoid. Still, he had come this far . . . "Now let me get this straight— You're going to give me money for just a little of my DNA, and then at the end of a month I get this identical clone of myself who will do all the work to earn all my money for me, while I spend all my time doing whatever the hell I please? For the entire rest of my life?"

"Succinctly put."

"Sucks is *right*! I don't fall for stuff that sounds too good to be true. This has got to be some sort of a scam, like those 'Earn a thousand dollars stuffing envelopes' ads."

"Think of it this way, Mister Michaels—I mean Calvin."

"Let's keep this on 'Mister Michaels' terms until I trust you more."

"Very well then, Mister Michaels." Wright continued on as smoothly as a snake slithering into its burrow. "Look around you. Can an unsuccessful business afford to rent this office, in this building? Look at me—do I appear to you to be a unsuccessful person?"

Calvin had to admit that he could get used to the lifestyle these surroundings and Wright's clothing and accessories indicated.

"Why not *be* one of the people who places ads such as mine, instead of needing to read and responding to them? *Place*, Mister Michaels. You need never again be one of the *respondents* of the world. Take the necessary action now to be in a situation where you are the one to *place* the ad."

Wright slid a piece of paper across his desk toward Calvin. The room was so still that Calvin could hear the hiss the paper made as it slid to a stop beneath the pen he was holding.

Calvin glanced down at the tablet on his lap that he had brought with him to take notes, secret messages to himself to catch the con man at his own game. Calvin was shrewd. He knew if he asked enough questions, and asked them again and

again in various different ways, he would get the salesman
to trip himself up; to reveal the traps in his memorized spiel
that were designed to ensnare the money-hungry, the fame-
hungry . . . the time-hungry.

The tired . . . the poor . . .

Calvin discovered that his hand had traced *Calvin Michaels*
across the signature line at the bottom of the page even before he
had consciously decided he should do so. He slid the paper back
across the desk toward the lab-coated salesman. At least Calvin
had assumed Wright was just a salesman for Homogenesis
Corporation. He might well be speaking to one of the doctors
who actually created these clones. Wouldn't *that* be —

"Shit!"

Calvin's hands were shaking so badly that he had to retype
the number on the telephone keypad three times before he
finally got the correct number as listed on the Homogenesis
Corporation's business card.

. . . brrr . . . brrr . . . brrr . . .

"Bloody *hell* — I can't even leave a voice mail! *Somebody* dead
or alive *answer* this damn thing already!"

"Homogenesis Corporation."

Finally!

"I'd like to speak to a Mister Wright, please? I believe he's one
of your salesmen. That's W-R-I-G-H-T."

"There is no Mister Wright in our employ, Sir. Perhaps you
misunderstood the name of the person you spoke with. If you'd
like me to connect you to our Human Resources De — "

"*No*, dammit! I know I didn't hear 'Wright' wrong!"

The woman from Homogenesis was unable to completely
muffle her chuckle, which infuriated Calvin even further. "I
need to talk to the person who gave me my contract. He said his
name was '*Mister Wright*'." Calvin enunciated, speaking slowly
as if to a child. "I heard him distinctly — I even saw it printed on
the contract he handed me. I signed it, right there at his desk,
about a month and a half ago. I'm looking at my copy of it right
here in front of me! He was definitely one of your employees
when I was at your offices. How the hell long do people work at

your place, anyway?"

The voice at the other end of the line continued to speak with robotic patience, infuriating Calvin even further. "Sir, our Human Resources Department can put you in touch with—"

"*Look*, lady. I can't even leave my house. I've got cops, FBI, every law enforcement agency that exists looking for me right now, only it's not me they're looking for—it's your *damn clone*! Your Mister . . . *Wright*, or whatever the hell he's calling himself now, wherever he's hiding himself—probably off drinking mai tais somewhere with my wife!—never gave me all the facts. He never made it clear to me in all his glowing terms that this wonderful *clone* your company was going to supply for me would have everything I've got *except* a soul! You've created a fucking *sociopath*, and you make it look just like *me*!! You've made *me* into a sociopath, as far as the world is concerned! That bastard with my face is going around robbing, raping, and basically doing whatever the hell it *wants* to and leaving *my* fingerprints, *my* hair, *my* DNA all *over* the place! So the cops aren't going after *it*, they're going after *me*! Because there's *no damn record* that the thing was ever created, except in your files! Now, I want your damn Mister Wright, or whoever has charge of my files there, to notify the authorities that you people created that thing out of my DNA, and that it isn't me! The *original* me, I mean!"

"You want us to tell the police there are two of you."

"*Yes!*"

"And risk the credibility of the Homogenesis Corporation."

"Wha . . . ?"

At first he mistook the pounding he heard in the background for the blood his overtaxed heart had been thrusting through his system with deadly force for the past six weeks. Then he realized that it was the butt of a policeman's gun hammering against his front door causing the racket. He hoped that door was solid wood. He'd never checked thoroughly enough before he bought the house.

He never checked anything thoroughly enough before he bought into it.

"There! Do you hear that?! I can't even call the cops on you people! Those *are* the cops! They'll drag me away! Now if you'll promise to explain everything to them, I'll let them in and put them on the phone."

"Explain, Sir?" The voice at the other end of the line was cold, impersonal. He might as well have been talking to a machine.

"Explain to them that it's not really me they're after! That I wasn't the one who did all that stuff. That there are two of us, that one of us was created by your company, and that your company made a mistake! You gave me a defective clone! Instead of creating somebody who was responsible, an exact copy of me like your ad said, you created some sort of Frankenstein's monster that's running around doing whatever the hell it pleases! *I* don't go running around the city after work mugging people in the park and raping everything in a skirt! So how can you say in your sales pitch that what you gave me is an exact duplicate of *me*?!"

Meanwhile, the pounding at the front door had stopped, replaced by an eerie quiet. Where the hell were they now? Walking around his house, looking into all the windows, trying to see if they could spot him inside, no doubt. Well, good luck to them; he'd shut and latched all the windows and closed all the drapes—even covered the block glass windows in the bathroom and basement with newspaper.

Calvin had always considered himself to be a thorough man; always covered all the bases. But that was before all this happened. That was one of the things that had made him such an *invaluable* employee, as his boss had told him when he cut back his hours and cut off his benefits so that he had to try to find a higher paying, second job. Not only could they not give him the raise he asked for, they would very much appreciate if he could be on call during his off hours to put in some unpaid overtime!

"Don't you wish there were two of you?" Calvin's secretary had said to him when he'd returned to his office.

He did, at the time.

But not anymore.

Something thumped against the door—a soft dull thud like the Sunday newspaper would make when it struck against the wood. Aha—so they *hadn't* left! Shrewd bastards. They thought they'd lie low, and he'd be stupid enough to open the door to check if they'd gone, and they'd have him. You should live so long, you bastards! He thought. That's why I used to be a Vice-President of Product Development and you've always been human bloodhounds. Because I can have all the angles covered, and you can't see past your own noses.

Uh-huh—and how many angles did you have covered when you signed that contract? His rational mind asked him. How did you get yourself into this situation? And, most importantly, how did you not see this coming?

"Sir," the mechanical voice on the telephone continued, "The Homogenesis Corporation takes pride in providing an exact physical reproduction of the DNA provided by its customers. We spare no expense in research and development, and it was only after continuous successful reproductions that we began offering our services to the public as a benefit to humankind." She sounded as though she was reading directly from their Annual Report.

"*Benefit to humankind??!!*" Calvin screamed, then guiltily looked around and listened to see if he had been loud enough to prick the ears of the bloodhounds lurking outside. He heard nothing but the sound of his own blood pulsing through his head. Taking a deep breath to calm himself, he continued: "How can you say these . . . *things* you make are 'benefits to humankind' when they're out there committing more crimes than the worst criminals in prison? At least *mine* sure as hell is—I can't even switch on the damn *news* at night without seeing my fucking face plastered all over the screen! He's turned me into Public Enemy Number One! I can't even leave my house to get something to eat, and that bastard is somehow able to elude everybody who's looking for him. Everybody but *me*, that is, because when I finally find him I'm gonna' set your precious Homogenesis research back fifty years with what I'm gonna' do to that thing! You just wait and see!"

"Which won't solve your problem."

"What?"

"Apparently, you haven't thought your actions through, if you don't mind my saying so. Destroying the evidence won't solve your problem, Sir. Right now he's your only alibi."

That much was true. How could Calvin convince anyone there were two of him if he beat his other self to an unrecognizable pulp? "Some alibi he's making for me if he's hiding god knows where!"

"At least he still exists. If you do what you're threatening to do, you'll be destroying your only alibi."

"Let them get his DNA off his dead body and test it! *Then* they'll know it wasn't me!"

"How so? Even if you manage to destroy our creation and they see you both with their own eyes, you will only be able to give evidence that you were not the one committing the crimes *by your word alone*. How will they be sure that our creation isn't the innocent party? They'll be presented with two identical sets of DNA—one living, one dead. How do you think they'll save face? Who will they want to prosecute, to exact revenge for these terrible crimes you say our product is committing?"

"I '*say*' your product is committing? Lady, don't you *watch the news*?! Do you really think that's me out there, deciding to go on a rampage all of a sudden?"

How would she know for a fact that the photo on the television and in the newspapers was actually a clone—sure as hell no one else was recognizing that! His ex-wife was going around telling anyone who stuck a microphone in her face that he always was a little crazy, and it was only time before she knew he'd snap from the stresses of his job. That's right—you tell 'em, baby. Go around acting like you were living on air when you were married to me and all the work I was doing was just for my own benefit. Don't tell 'em how you cleaned out all my accounts. How ninety-nine percent of my stress was because of you. The only time I was 'a little crazy' was when I said "I do." What I should've "done" was got a dog if I wanted company—and loyalty.

"Sir, where is your clone now? Do you have any idea?"

Good fucking question, Calvin thought. He'd be all over the fucking walls if he was anywhere I knew to get at him. The pounding was beginning again, this time at the back door. Had they seen shadows of him moving around inside the house as he was holding this pointless conversation with the automaton at Homogenesis?

"Lady, if I *knew* where the thing was right now, *why* would I be standing here, trying to get some answers out of your fu— . . . out of your *Corporation*?" He pronounced the last with all the sarcasm he could muster, all the while knowing how ineffective it was going to be. Well, he was entitled to some little satisfaction.

"Sir, may I discuss your problem with my superiors and get back to you shortly? If you would leave a number at which you can be reached . . ."

"555-6972. The number should be in your records, if your 'corporation' even *keeps* legitimate records. Don't worry about my missing your call. I'll be waiting, right here by the phone. *I* sure as hell can't go anywhere."

"How do we solve the Calvin Michaels dilemma?" The secretary asked her supervisor, who had been standing behind her desk listening to the entire exchange over the speakerphone.

"Fortunately we 'tag' the genes, unbeknownst to either the clones *or* the donors. It was the one requirement to obtain the secret government funding that I was happy to comply with. The government's paranoia over the possibility of another country's cloning the President fit in perfectly with our plans, for once. All I have to do is look up his number, type it into the computer and it'll instantly track the clone's location, like a GPS system for humans. Or as close to human as we're able to make them." Wright smiled icily. As he spoke, Wright signaled an assistant to do just that. The young man nodded and left the room, without a word exchanged between them.

"But if we tell Mister Michaels where his clone is, he'll either report it to the police or make it his personal vendetta to destroy the clone himself. Either alternative is going to bring negative attention to Homogenesis."

"There's not much he can do on his own now. You heard him—he's trapped in his own house."

 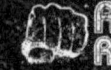 

"Eventually, the police will either break down his door or he will give up and answer the door of his own accord and tell everything to the police. The police may well already be there in his house when I call him back, and I'm sure he would put them on the phone and insist that we explain to them. Or he'll allow the police to listen to everything I say. He also has his copy of our contract as further evidence."

The assistant returned to the office and, after handing Wright a single sheet of paper, turned and left the room as unobtrusively as he arrived.

"No point in traumatizing the gentleman any further, Miss Winters. I don't think you will need to make that return call after all. Nor should you, probably."

"Why not?"

"I have a report on the location of the clone. The signal is coming from inside Calvin Michaels's house. Right next to his telephone."

Susan E. Abramski "Double Jeopardy" is my thirtieth work to see publication since a first-draft transcription of a nightmare I called "The Cabinet Of Living Things" appeared in the first publication I submitted it to: *The Monthly . . . Bulletin* #67 in August of 1996. (In 2000 a lengthier version appeared in *Outer Darkness* #21.) Before that time, I rarely even read horror, let alone thought to write it almost exclusively. Since then, during a time of nonstop catch-up horror reading which had also seen a marriage and move from Chicago IL to a small town in Northern California, my work has appeared in *Penny Dreadful*, *Crossroads*, *Outer Darkness*, *MindMares*, *Extremes 1* CD-ROM, *Microhorror*, *Dark Planet*, *Eyes* and *The Midnight Gallery* among others—though never again in first draft form!

PULP MODERN

pulp-modern.blogspot.com

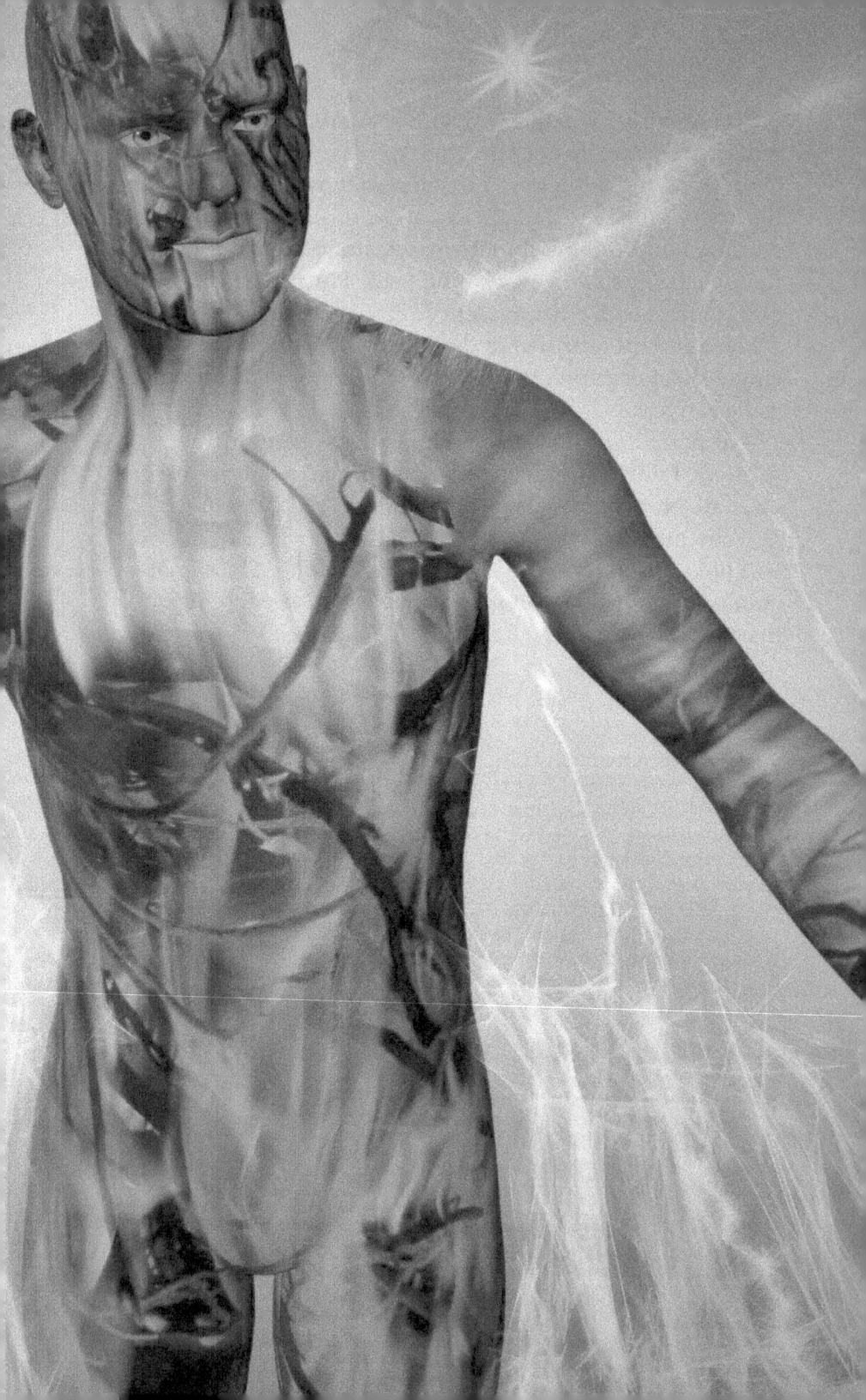

An amazing human flaw is the undying
temptation to explain the unexplainable.

Godhead
by J. Robert Kane

Jaden Baker focused his thoughts and sent a
tendril of white-hot energy out into the night.
It collapsed, upon contact with its target, into a
seething ball of flame.

The unlucky young woman, who'd been
jogging along a well-lit and well-populated area
of the park, slowed to a stop. She looked down,
examined herself. Her reaction might have been
comical, under less fatal circumstances. Her fiery
form regarded itself and its new state with a
complete lack of understanding. The fact that she
was on fire seemed, for the time, to bother her
less than the fact that she didn't understand *why*.

Her reaction, Baker knew from experience, was
more common than not. People simply don't
expect to spontaneously combust, and when
they do the shock can be paralyzing. Eventually,
though, they all scream. The pain overcomes
the disbelief to become the center of the victim's
consciousness. By that point, any people in the
immediate area are usually screaming also.
When at last the victim falls, he or she bends first
at the knees, and invariably falls flat on his or
her face.

Baker's latest victim did just this. Her slight
body twitched and jerked. Her skin, hair
and jogging-suit smoldered. The shrieks and
screams of the lookers-on receded into moans

and then sobs. The sobs collapsed into a low, droning chorus of whimpers.

He'd seen enough. And more importantly, the pressure was gone . . . for now.

Godhead. That, Jaden Baker knew, was his saving grace. It was the reason that he was no murderer, the reason he had no stain on his soul. No longer was he bound by the rules that govern mortal men. He'd been . . . *elevated*.

Jaden Baker's apotheosis had occurred on March Eleventh, Two-Thousand Four. He'd been riding the subway home from work when, unprovoked, a disturbed passenger (it would later be discovered that she suffered bipolar-depression and was off her medication) jabbed a nine-inch knitting-needle directly into his eye. The experience had been every bit as excruciating and terrifying as one might imagine.

It had also proven the most significant event in his life. Because as he stood screaming and holding his eye-socket—as he wondered whether it would be better to leave the needle as it was, or to try and remove it—he felt a presence surround, and then *fill* him.

At first it was just the single presence . . . a single *consciousness*. Once the presence permeated him, though, Baker had quickly become aware of others around him—presences unseen to the human eye, but no less tangible for that . . . .

"He's your guy."

Detective Sanchez looked less than convinced. He fixed the other man with a glare usually reserved for suspects in the interrogation room. "You're sure?"

Jaden nodded. "I'm positive."

"Can you prove it?"

"That's your job, detective." Baker indicated the check-register the detective had taken from his drawer, had placed on his shit-heap of a desk. "But he's your guy. The usual fee, I take it."

Sanchez opened the register, went about writing out payment. "You know, if it was up to me, I wouldn't even let you in the front door."

"You don't say. I would never have guessed."

"You're a con-man, Mr. Baker. I've seen your type before."

I sincerely doubt that . . ., the earthbound god thought.

He wanted to sleep. And, if sleep evaded him, he wanted to curl up with a good novel, or find an old black-and-white movie on television. There were times when he felt so . . . *human*.

There was business to be done, though. Always, there was business. He was on a mission now; he'd been plucked from his mortal condition and made to understand the universe at a higher level of description. This, he knew, had not happened so that he could read the newest Stephen King book, or watch Cagney in *Angels with Dirty Faces* for the thousandth time.

How gratifying it would be, he thought, if he could choose his *own* targets. He fantasized about it, sometimes. To focus his mind and burn the Detective Sanchez's of the world would be satisfying, to say the least. Being more than human now, though, Baker recognized the *human-ness* of such lower thoughts. As such, he pushed them aside.

He had work to do; He would sleep when it was done.

When he'd been human, Jaden Baker had assumed that people were, for the most part, good. He'd taken comfort in the idea that most of the thoughts being radiated out into the universe were positive, hopeful ones—or, at the least, neutral ones.

Upon achieving godhead, he'd quickly learned the truth. That fateful day in March of Two-Thousand-Four, as he'd pondered his seemingly imminent death—as he was mistaking the presences filling and surrounding him for his guides to the afterlife—something had happened to his brain . . . to his *mind*.

The change was heralded by an audible pop from deep within his own consciousness. immediately following that, Baker had experienced an acute sensation of connectedness to his environment. Suddenly, he could see the wonder of mathematics in everything around him. It had been both beautiful and terrifying; awe-inspiring and anxiety-inducing.

And then the voices had started.

He'd been so focused on the incorporeal beings with which he was suddenly communing, that he'd at first taken the voices to be theirs. These voices were strange, though . . . disjointed. They were trains-of-thought given voice.

. . . my God, what do I do? If that bitch gets anywhere near me I'll . . .

. . . fuck. I won't be getting home in time for . . .

. . . so much blood. My God, I hope he doesn't have AIDS . . .

. . . should be videoing this, the news might pay for . . .

. . . this is SICK! This is better than DEATHBRINGER FOUR . . .

. . . poor man, someone should help him . . .

The disappointment he'd felt, upon realizing that what he was hearing were the thoughts of his fellow passengers, had been almost too much to bear. For just a second, Baker forgot completely about the needle protruding from his eye-socket. He wanted to be angry at his fellow passengers, he'd wanted to hate them for the things they were thinking—for the things that had preoccupied them all as they'd watched him suffer.

The *others* were still with him, though. They soothed him wordlessly; they reassured him. He found that, in their presence, it was impossible to stay angry. The usefulness of anger as a shield against sadness was made painfully clear to Baker, and he fell to his knees, clutching the handrail for support.

Another victim burned alive. As always, the experience left Baker feeling beleaguered in body, mind and spirit. The echoes of the screams of the dead reverberated in his mind. At heightened moments of awareness, such as were necessary to utilize his pyrokinetic talent, he could more than hear his victim's tortured thoughts . . . he could *feel* them.

There were moments of doubt.

Jaden Baker was an educated man, and the idea that he'd become a god (or a demigod, or a deity of any sort) was a lot to process.

The pyro-kinesis, he knew, might possibly be explained away by the brain-damage he'd suffered. He'd done research, and found one or two "documented" cases of people who'd demonstrated exactly that dubious talent after having suffered massive brain-trauma.

And if the pyro-kinesis might be explained away by the brain-damage he'd suffered on that fateful day, so too might the telepathy.

On long, creeping nights such as this, when his mind turned to such things, Baker felt the ominous specter of guilt. It was deep and somehow attractive; it bespoke fathoms of soul-crushing anguish . . .

Peace, child . . .

The beings with whom Jaden Baker had communed since his apotheosis did not speak, even within his mind. Rather, this was the feeling that the alien consciousness was radiating into his own being. *Peace, child . . .*

His sense of identity refreshed, the earthbound god relaxed.

Jaden Baker watched his latest victim collapse at the knees and fall forward. He experienced the old man's anguish, his terror.

There was a sharp *pop* then, not unlike the one he'd heard when he'd been stabbed in the eye. His telepathic bond with the burning man was broken. He turned and saw an approaching police officer. The cop was holding his gun over his head; as Baker turned, the cop leveled the weapon.

"Stop right there! Don't you move!"

The officer approached with caution. He was about twenty feet away, and closing.

Baker, startled at having been identified, broke and ran. There was another *pop*. The fleeing god was nearly to the woods surrounding the park. From there, he could disappear.

Just as he reached the wood-line, though, something stabbed Baker in the left shoulder. A fraction of a second later, another *pop*. He spun on his heel, but kept his feet, and fled into the natural cover.

Thirty minutes later, Jaden Baker walked into his house, exhausted and wounded. He sat in the darkness of his living room, forgiving the officer who'd shot him, and considering the implications of this troubling new development. He was shot, and bleeding. It wasn't a mortal wound, by any means, but then he was not a mortal man . . .

I am the god of fire . . .

But gods shouldn't bleed, should they?

He must have fallen asleep as he pondered this, because he came abruptly awake as the front-door of his small house burst, frame and all, into his living room. Amidst a shower of splinters and broken glass, five heavily-armed men in tactical gear ran through the new opening.

"Do you know where you are?"

Baker nodded. "Mercy-General."

The mountain of a nurse nodded, smiled. "Good. And can you tell me your name?"

I am the fire-god, and my name is my own . . .

"Jaden Baker," he heard himself say.

"Okay," she made a note on her clipboard. "Very good." She leaned forward to check his shoulder dressing. Her enormous tits brushed his arm and he felt a decidedly mortal urge. "Are you comfortable?" She straightened. Her cheeks were flushed.

The earthbound god concentrated on not getting an erection. He wore nothing but a thin sheet. "Yes, thank you."

"Okay, well, if—"

Baker sat up. "Wait, I'm sorry . . . can you turn that up?"

The nurse narrowed her eyes, but she walked over and raised the volume on the television.

"In his basement laboratory in the Mind and Consciousness Center, the doctor you're about to meet says he's found a way to simulate the 'God Experience.'" The news anchor paused for dramatic effect. "By employing a small magnetic charge to a specific area of the brain, he is able to create a sense of being in the presence of the divine. We talk to the good doctor, and to a number of his test subjects . . ."

The weight was smothering, goliath. It was enough, Baker had to concede, to crush a god. Because first there was the weight of realizing that, despite the feelings of assurance being generated still by the consciousness inside of him, he, Jaden Baker, was not a god. What he'd experienced that day had not been an apotheosis, but a catastrophic brain injury that had affected his right temporal lobe. Now, his feeling of communion with the divine could be explained away as rationally as his other godlike powers.

What was worse, though (and much worse, because Baker had never wanted to be a god—it had been both a bitterly sad and an emotionally painful experience,) was the guilt. It was staggering, the size of it. If he'd had the immortal life of a true deity, it might take him ten-thousand years to process it all.

It wasn't at all easy, Jaden Baker thought, falling back to earth.

Detective Sanchez stepped into Baker's hospital room. He removed a handkerchief from his breast pocket, held it over his mouth and nose.

The smell was overwhelming, but it was the sight of the corpse that made the seasoned detective's stomach flip-flop in his abdomen. Burned beyond recognition, the remains could barely be construed as having been human. All over the crime-scene (because really, what else could you call this?) bits of white foam clung to organic evidence and burned bedding. Some good Samaritan had tried the fire-extinguisher, apparently.

Still holding the hanky over his lower face with his left hand, Sanchez made the sign of the cross with his right.

He lowered the handkerchief. "I guess I was wrong about you, Baker. You weren't a conman after all." He turned to leave, glanced once over his shoulder. "But what the hell were you? What sort of *demon*?"

Author's Note: There is no scientific evidence to support that either pyro-kinesis or telepathy exist, or are even possible. There are many documented cases, though, of catastrophic brain injury resulting in all manner of strange experience and/or behavior, ranging from drastic changes in personality to severely distorted perceptions of time. The "God Helmet" is real.

J. Robert Kane is a type-setter and machine operator who writes horror and science-fiction. As a songwriter, his work has appeared on national television commercials and in videos for Cold Spring Harbor Laboratory's Double-Helix Award. He earned a bachelor's degree in American History from SUNY Empire State College, where he received the Joseph L. Mancino Scholarship there, and volunteered in the campus writing lab. Hailing from Long Island, New York, Kane lives with his longtime love Rebecca.

Hardboiled, Noir and Gold Medals:

Essays on Crime Fiction Writers from the '50s through the '90s
by Rick Ollerman

"Reading HARDBOILED, NOIR AND GOLD MEDALS is like spending a "brandy and cigars" evening with a close, trusted and knowledgeable friend as he shares the fruits of his research and the many joys of reading crime fiction. It belongs on the shelf of every crime fiction fan–as both a valuable addition to and perhaps the cornerstone of their reference books."

Alan Cranis, *Bookgasm*

"Reading one of Rick Ollerman's essays is like sitting in a master class on the writer. Having all of the essays in one collection is like getting a master's degree. This is an important book and a must-have for anybody who cares about good criticism, about the writers discussed, and about crime fiction in general."

Bill Crider, author

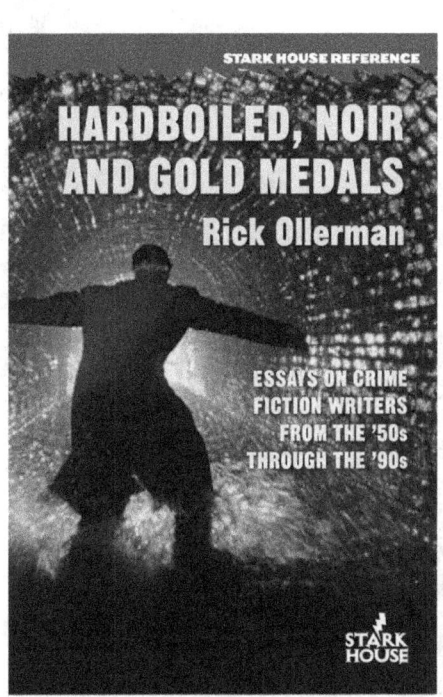

$17.95   296 pages
978-1-944520-32-8

STARK HOUSE PRESS
1315 H Street, Eureka, CA 95501
707-498-3135 www.StarkHousePress.com

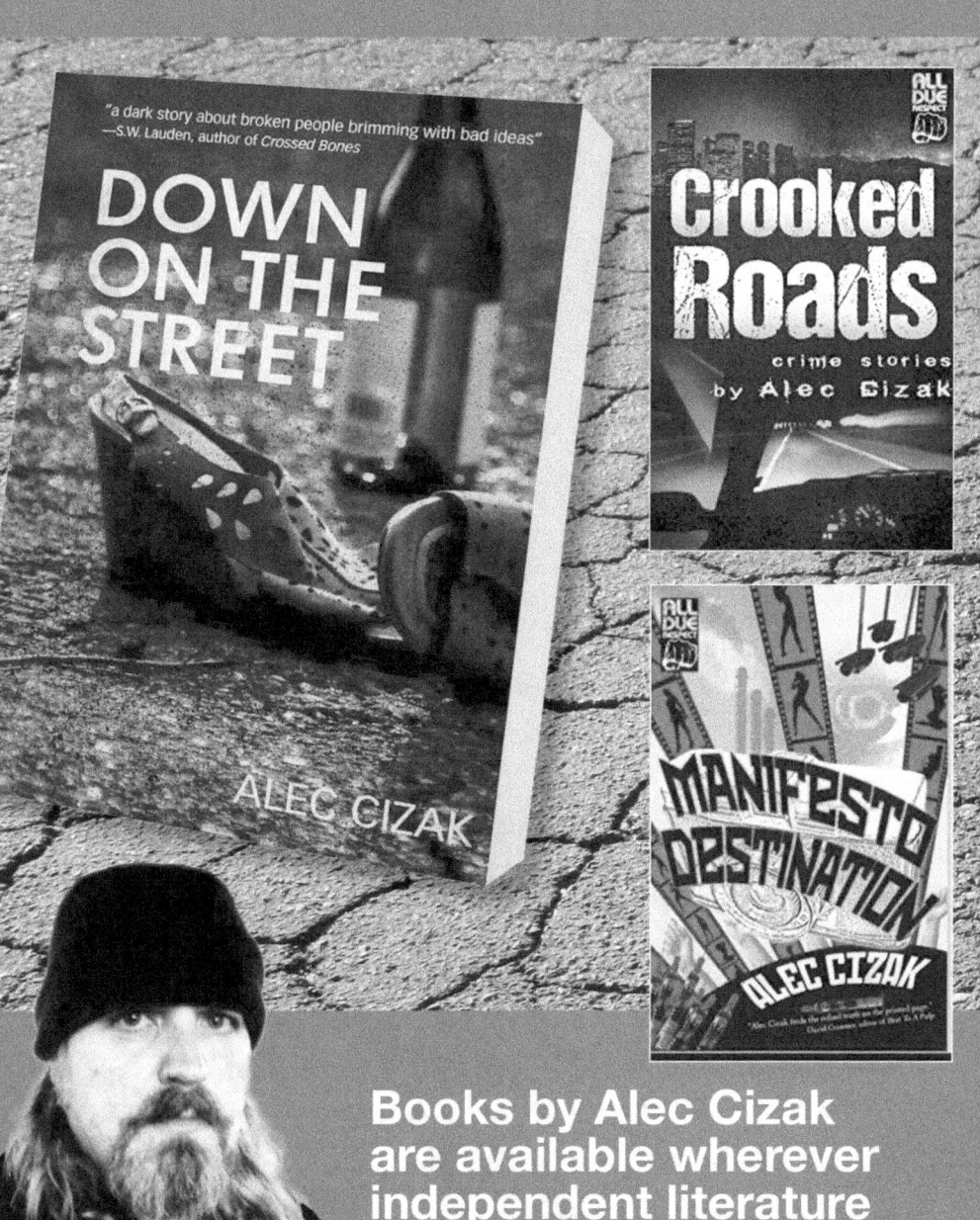

UNSPLATTERPUNK! 2

EDITED BY **DOUGLAS J. OGUREK**

OUT
MARCH 2018

INTRODUCTION BY
RAFE MCGREGOR

**SUBMISSIONS BY
28 FEBRUARY 2018**
theakersquarterlyfiction.
blogspot.com

THEAKER'S QUARTERLY FICTION

Contact
Get the latest news and announcements at <pulp-modern. blogspot> and <facebook.com/pulpmodern> Post feedback on Facebook or write to <pulpmodern@yahoo.com>

Links
Tom Andes <tomandes.com>
Marc E. Fitch <marcfitch.com>
Matthew X. Gomez <mxgomez.wordpress.com>
Preston Lang <prestonlangbooks.com>
Robert Petyo <twitter.com/robertpetyo>
Charles Roland <charlesrolandauthor.com>
Jim Thomsen <jimthomsencreative.com>
Bob Vojtko <facebook.com/bob.vojtko.7>

Get a free ebook of *The Digest Enthusiast* book one on Magzter when you sign up for the Larque Press mailing list. More info at <LarquePress.com> For a daily dose of digest magazine news and history visit the Digest Magazines blog at <LarquePress.com>

Advertisers' Index